MORE WILD CAMP TALES

Mike Blakely

Republic of Texas Press

Library of Congress Cataloging-in-Publication Data

Blakely, Mike.
   More wild camp tales / Mike Blakely.
      p. cm.
   ISBN 1-55622-392-7 (pbk.)
   1. Tales--Texas.   2. Texas--History--Miscellanea.   3. Texas--
   Social life and customs.   I. Title.
   GR110.T5B55   1995
   398.2'09764--dc20   95-636
                                     CIP

Republic of Texas Press is an imprint of Wordware Publishing, Inc.
No part of this book may be reproduced in any form or by
any means without permission in writing from
Wordware Publishing, Inc.

Printed in the United States of America

ISBN1-55622-392-7
10 9 8 7 6 5 4 3 2 1
9511

All inquiries for volume purchases of this book should be addressed
to Wordware Publishing, Inc., at 1506 Capital Avenue, Plano, Texas
75074. Telephone inquiries may be made by calling:
(214) 423-0090

Contents

Part 3
WILD WEST

Part 4
WILD CRITTERS

Part 5
WILDEST TALES

Introduction

As I went about the enjoyable task of gathering material for this second volume of Wild Camp Tales from the hundreds of newspaper and magazine pieces I had written over the years, I was reminded of something Bigfoot Wallace once told about raconteuring.

Bigfoot was a legend in his own time in Texas, and an accomplished spinner of far-fetched fabrications. He went back to Virginia to visit his people once, and they threw a big fandango for him. His kinfolk got to asking him about Texas, and he went on about huge herds of buffalo and mustangs and such:

"At first I answered truthfully all the questions they asked me; but when I found they evidently doubted some of the stories I told them which were facts, then I branched out and gave them some whoppers. These they swallowed down without gagging."

The point is that some of the wild tales in this book are undoubtably true, some questionable as to their veracity, and some intentional "windies." I wrote these short features for many different publications, intended for a variety of readerships. I have tried to establish a tone in each of these tales that will suggest to the reader how far the blanket has been stretched, if any, in the telling or the retelling of the tale.

As the great historian/folklorist J. Frank Dobie once wrote in one of his thousands of heroically comprehensive footnotes: "If one man does not tell a story—*as a story*—the way it should be told, the next man is under artistic obligations to improve it." (The italics are mine.)

Dobie possessed a gift for moving between fact and fabrication without ever losing the distinction between the two. Others have not been so gifted or so disciplined. As Bigfoot would remind us, the taller the tale, the more folks tend to want to believe in it. This holds true for the teller of the tale, as well as the listener.

One of the most famous liars from the Old West was a fellow called Lyin' Jack. His favorite story was a yarn about a fabulous elk hunt in which he killed a bull with antlers fifteen feet wide. He told everyone that he kept those antlers in the loft of his cabin.

One evening Lyin' Jack showed up at a saloon, and the boys began badgering him for a windy.

"No, boys," said Jack, "I'm through. For years I've been tellin' these lies—told 'em so often I got to believin' 'em myself. That story of mine about the elk with the fifteen-foot horns is what cured me. I told about that elk so often that I knowed the place I killed it. One night I lit a candle and crawled up in the loft to view the horns—and I'm damned if they weren't there!"

With that caution in mind, I invite the reader to conjure the image of a crackling camp fire. Imagine the likes of Bigfoot Wallace, Noah Smithwick, Charlie Siringo, and J. Frank Dobie ringing the fire. Sit yourself among them and listen. Some will tell you a story the way it happened. Some will tell you a story *as a story*. If they didn't respect your ability to judge the difference, they wouldn't have invited you to "roast your shins" at their fire in the first place.

Mike Blakely
Rancho Quien Sabe
Burnet County, Texas

PART 1

WILD
TEXANS

BIGFOOT WALLACE

William A. "Bigfoot" Wallace got his start in Texas as a hunter. For a year he killed deer along San Pedro creek to sell to the residents of San Antonio. In 1839 he moved to the future site of Austin and provided game meat for the workers who were building the capital city. Deer, bear, turkey, and buffalo abounded in the area. He could earn seventy dollars for a load of turkey and bear. On one occasion, Wallace accidentally stampeded a herd of bison down Congress Avenue, which was at the time marked off only with stakes. It was one of the tamer adventures of his long life.

Aside from his reputation as an exceptionally intrepid hunter, woodsman, Texas Ranger, scout, soldier, and Indian fighter, Bigfoot became known as a great wit and a practiced raconteur. Concerning the source of his famous nickname, for example, he appears to have spread several different versions himself. It seems that every time someone asked him how he earned the nickname, he simply made up a new tale.

One of Wallace's stories says that he and a dozen or so other Texas Rangers were sent out on a hunting detail to provide meat for their ranger unit. They left New Braunfels and rode many miles up the Guadalupe looking for game. Then one night Indians snuck into camp and stole all their horses.

To rejoin their main outfit downstream, the rangers built a raft and loaded their saddles, the game they had bagged, and their other trappings aboard. Wallace and another ranger guided the makeshift vessel down the river while the rest of the rangers walked. To keep his boots dry, Wallace took them off and put them on top of the cargo.

The raft hit a stretch of rapids and overturned some-where downstream. Neither ranger was injured, but Wallace lost his boots. He became footsore from plodding on without them. Finally the rangers killed a maverick for food and used the hide to fashion shoes for Wallace's feet. The frontier cobblers made the footgear none too stylish and a few sizes too big.

When the rangers finally reached New Braunfels, the German settlers there couldn't help noticing Wallace's over-sized rawhide shoes. They laughed, pointed, and kept uttering something in their native language. When one of the rangers asked for a translation, the Germans said that they were calling Wallace "Bigfoot" and the name stuck.

But that's just one version of the origin of Bigfoot's nick-name. Wallace told someone else that he earned his sobriquet while living in Austin. There was a Waco Indian in that area named Chief Bigfoot. He was a huge brute—some said 300 pounds—with a size fourteen foot. He was constantly making a nuisance of himself in that area.

One night the daughter of one of Wallace's neighbors saw the outline of an unidentified peeping tom looking through her window. The next morning her angry father tracked a pair of huge moccasin prints to Wallace's front door. Wallace had pretty big feet himself and often wore moccasins, so the father accused him of invading his daugh-ter's privacy. Wallace planted his own foot inside the Indian's track with room to spare and thereby proved that he had not made the footprints. Yet, before the day passed, everyone in town was calling him "Bigfoot" after the noto-rious Waco warrior. (The crafty Indian had made a tremendous leap from Wallace's door to a grassy spot in an attempt to pin the foul deed on Wallace.)

Bigfoot told John C. Duval an entirely different story about his distinctive handle. Duval's book *The Adventures of Bigfoot Wallace* says the famous frontiersman acquired his name while being held prisoner in Mexico City after his capture by Mexican soldiers at the 1842 battle of Mier.

Some of the citizens of Mexico City felt sorry for Wallace and the other Texas prisoners and provided them all with much needed shoes. Wallace wore a size twelve but a search of every store in town didn't even produce an eleven. Finally, his amused Mexican benefactors had a pair specially made for him. So, according to Duval, the nickname "Bigfoot" was first spoken in the Spanish language.

Wallace once said he didn't mind the name "Bigfoot" because it was better than some of the alternatives, like "Lying" Wallace. It's obvious that he didn't have to stretch the truth much to awe his listeners.

It is an established fact that Bigfoot Wallace served time as a prisoner in Mexico City. It is also known that he lived among Indians at Austin and in many other areas of Texas. He could have ridden rafts down the Guadalupe River on any number of hunting trips. Because his adventures were so numerous and thrilling, it's possible that a little truth exists in all of Bigfoot's tales about the origin of his appellation.

JOHN PARKER

Many students of Texas history know the story of Cynthia Ann Parker, girl captive of the Comanche, wife of Chief Peta Nacona, mother of Chief Quanah Parker. Relatively little has been written, however, on the life of Cynthia Ann's brother, John Parker, though he also suffered as an Indian captive, lived among Comanches for many years, and outlived his legendary sister by forty-four years.

Indians raided Fort Parker, Texas, on May 19, 1836, taking scalps and carrying away five captives, including nine-year-old Cynthia Ann and six-year-old John Parker. The Indians separated the Parker children forever after three days. Cynthia Ann went on to her fabled life with the Quahadi Comanches while John fell into relative obscurity among the Kiowa band.

After holding John Parker for six years, the Indians ransomed him back to whites in 1842. But John did not easily revert to the ways of the white man. He had become Comanche. He soon returned to the Indians, ostensibly to search for Cynthia Ann.

John became a Comanche warrior and began participating in raids along the Rio Grande and into Mexico. On one raid south of the border, John's band captured a pretty Mexican girl of Aztec descent named Dona Maria.

John fell for the captive beauty and wanted her for his wife. Dona Maria had no inclination to resist. The kind treatment John assured her of made her devoted to him. The couple traveled north into Texas, to be married in the Comanche way at the end of the journey.

Then John's life was again changed forever when he came down with small pox on the trail north. The Indians feared an epidemic and quickly abandoned him on the plains to die. Dona Maria, however, would not leave her protector. She stayed with John and nursed him back to health.

Thereafter, John refused to have anything to do with the nomads who had cast him aside. He took Dona Maria back to Mexico and became a rancher and guide near the border. Those who knew him said his features looked like those of a Comanche warrior, though he had not a single drop of Indian blood in his veins.

During the Civil War, Parker, who still considered himself a Texan, joined a Mexican company of the Confederate army. He refused, however, to serve the Confederacy east of the Sabine River. He thought Texans should fight only on Texas soil. On the way back to Mexico he stayed with an uncle he had not seen since his capture in 1836.

Parker remained in Mexico after the war. He declined any more visits with his white relatives in Texas, even though Cynthia Ann had been recaptured from the Comanches in 1860 and was struggling to readjust to white civilization. She lost the struggle and died in 1871.

John did receive one visitor about 1880. His nephew, Chief Quanah Parker, last war chief of the Comanches, came to see him. Quanah had ended warfare with whites and now led his tribe in accepting the white man's ways.

Parker far outlived his famous sister and even his nephew, Quanah, who died in 1911. His extraordinary life ended on his ranch in Mexico in 1915.

THOMPSON AND FISHER

Texas history has its share of good men, bad men, and a few who couldn't make up their minds. The paths of two outlaws-turned-lawmen crossed in San Antonio in 1884— and ended there. King Fisher and Ben Thompson had each served time on both sides of jailhouse bars when they met.

Ben Thompson shot and wounded a playmate at age thirteen, and later killed a Frenchman in a knife duel fought in a darkened New Orleans icehouse. He fought for lost causes such as the Confederacy and Emperor Maximilian's Mexico before he returned to his Austin home.

Thompson served two years in prison for wounding his wife's brother with a gunshot. When released, he moved to Kansas to open a drinking and gambling establishment. He was fond of whiskey, games of chance, and gunplay himself.

Thompson returned to Austin, ran for city marshal twice, and won in 1879. Under the sure aim of Ben Thompson, Austin crime reached an unparalleled low. His skill with a handgun and his coolness under fire virtually ridded the city of violence.

In 1882 Thompson went on a pleasure trip to San Antonio where he shot and killed the owner of the Vaudeville Theater in a poker argument. He resigned as Austin's marshal but beat the murder charge.

Thompson then apparently decided to make up for all the law and order he had brought to Austin. He went on a drinking, gambling, and shooting spree, raising havoc in courtrooms, saloons, threaters, and in the newspaper office in Austin.

King Fisher had spent four months in prison by the age of sixteen. Returning from Huntsville, he hired out to ranchers in the lawless Nueces River territory to stop cattle rustling. Soon, however, Fisher started his own gang of rustlers. The Texas Rangers often arrested him, but he beat about a dozen murder charges and several lesser counts.

Always cordial to the ladies and a devoted family man, the handsome Fisher was a striking figure in his Mexican sombrero, red sash, and ivory-handled revolvers. He became so powerful and feared that he posted a sign on the road forking toward his ranch: "This is King Fisher's Road. Take the other."

After many arrests by the relentless Texas Rangers, King Fisher apparently decided to reform. He moved to Uvalde and became deputy sheriff. In 1884 he planned to run, unopposed, for Uvalde County Sheriff. That's when he met Ben Thompson.

Ben Thompson, 42, and King Fisher, 30, struck up an instant friendship. On March 11, 1884, Fisher accompanied Thompson to his old haunt in San Antonio—the Vaudeville Theater. The notorious and the infamous sauntered side-by-side, pistols on their hips, into the theater. As they crossed the threshold, a barrage of lead flew from assassins concealed in a theater box. Both Thompson and Fisher fell dead. Texans didn't know whether to mourn or celebrate their murders.

POST'S PLUVICULTURE

Remember kite-flying on gusty spring days? The fabric flapping with the stiff blasts, jerking against the string; the careening loops, zig-zags, and dives of your tethered flier; the wild whipping motions of its tail behind it, and the inevitable crash landings?

Now imagine launching that same bobbing, swooping kite with an extra string dangling thirty feet below it. To that string you tie a two-pound stick of dynamite, light the five-minute fuse, and run! Now you peel off enough string to reach the proper altitude for the blast. Too dangerous? That's what Charles W. Post decided. He had to find some other way of making rain.

Post came to Texas in 1886 for his health, yet somehow ended up playing with kites and dynamite. His successes in manufacturing farm machinery had made him wealthy, but overwork caused him to suffer from nervous disorders, as if dynamite on a kite string would not. His speculations in Fort Worth real estate and textile mills also brought him success and frequent "nervous breakdowns."

Post decided that coffee caused his ill health, so he invented a coffee substitute called "Postem Food Coffee." His genius in advertising and marketing caused such a demand for "Postem" that the inventor made a fortune. "Post Toasties," "Grape-Nuts," and other Post cereals followed. C.W. Post became a multimillionaire, and his nerves became steady enough to harness a dodging, bucking kite with dynamite.

Though Post also lived in Michigan, Connecticut, California, Illinois, and Washington, D.C., he held a special affinity for the Texas High Plains. In 1906 he bought 333 square miles of land along the Cap Rock, southeast of Lubbock, and a year later he founded Post, Texas.

C.W. Post did everything possible to provide his well-planned farming community with all its needs—even rain. Post remembered the Civil War as a boy—a heavy rain always seemed to follow a big battle. Post theorized that the sound waves or rising columns of air from the cannon fire caused moisture in the air to "precipitate," creating rainfall. He endeavored to go one better by flying dynamite hundreds of feet above the High Plains on kites.

After the kite experiment proved too dangerous, Post had his men set charges at various intervals of time and distance along the Cap Rock to imitate an artillery battle. In all, Post waged twenty-three "rain battles" between 1910 and 1913. His greatest success came in 1911, and he became convinced that he could "shoot up a rain" under almost any conditions. North Texas newspapers hailed Post's pluviculture in front-page, bold-face fashion, and reported that he had produced rain around the city of Post while other communities remained dry.

Oh, there were doubters—still are. But while C.W. Post lived, no one ever told him to go fly a kite. They knew he had a short fuse.

THE ARCHIVE WAR

Angelina Eberly had decided that Sam Houston lived to threaten the prosperity of her hotel business. San Felipe had seemed the logical location for the Declaration of Independence Convention, and Angelina's hotel there would have filled with leaders of a new republic. But Sam Houston suggested Washington-on-the-Brazos as a site for the convention, and Angelina's hotel became conspicuously vacant.

Just weeks later, Sam Houston, the general, led his retreating army through San Felipe and reduced the town to ashes to prevent Mexican troops from looting it. Angelina took it personally. She had no business to return to.

She went back into the hotel business in Austin, but Sam Houston, the president, still frustrated her efforts. He wanted the capital—and much of Angelina's clientele—moved to Washington-on-the-Brazos. He said Austin stood wide open to attacks by Mexicans and Indians. Houston had a point. Comanches had scalped some of the workmen constructing the first capitol building, and 1,000 Mexican troops had captured San Antonio in March 1842.

Still, Angelina complained when the president called an emergency session of Congress to convene in Houston instead of Austin. She railed when the president ordered the Texas Archives—the records of the Republic—taken from her city. But she rejoiced when a group of leading Austinites formed a vigilance committee to guard the archives and defy Houston's order.

Now, the "Archive War" remained a standoff on New Year's Eve. Angelina Eberly slept restlessly. What kind of prosperous new year could she expect with Sam Houston spoiling her every business venture? How she would love to spoil some scheme of his!

Angelina woke to a commotion down the street behind the Land Office building. Were the archives unguarded? She rushed from her hotel to the Land Office and saw twenty-six rangers, on a secret mission from Sam Houston, loading the archives into two wagons.

The hotel keeper sprinted half a block to Congress Avenue. She gripped the city's cannon, always loaded with grape shot in case of Indian attack. She whirled the six-pounder so the muzzle bore down on "Houston's henchmen." Angelina was no cannoneer, but she knew enough to touch torch to powder, and the big gun roared.

The rangers somehow escaped injury from the spray of metal but hastened from the site with the archives lest Angelina's aim improve. The cannon blast woke many of the vigilantes who mounted and followed the rangers east. At dawn, the vigilantes surrounded Houston's men and demanded the archives. The rangers, under Houston's orders to avoid bloodshed, surrendered the Republic's papers to Austin's citizens.

The archives remained in Austin and the capital returned the next year. Angelina Eberly won the honor of keeping the archives in her personal custody for a time. And she won the satisfaction of dealing Sam Houston a rare defeat.

BRITT JOHNSON

Former slave Britt Johnson was one of the most re-spected men on the northern Texas frontier. He earned his reputation as an Indian tracker, negotiator, and rescuer of Indian captives.

As a freedman, Britt Johnson worked for his former master, Allen Johnson, but also worked for a widow, Eliza-beth Fitzpatrick, and served as an orderly at Fort Belknap in Young County during the 1850s. The U.S. soldiers there recognized Britt as one of the best marksmen on the fron-tier.

For a couple of years, Britt visited Penateka Comanches at a nearby reservation, befriending their leaders and learn-ing some of their language. But the Indians abandoned the reservation in 1858 and went on the warpath for the next several years.

Britt was away from his home at widow Fitzpatrick's ranch on October 13, 1864, when 600-700 Comanches and Kiowas attacked. The widow's daughter tried to hold them off with a gun and was killed. Two Indians killed Britt's oldest son in an argument over who had captured him.

The war party attacked several other settlers in the area, killed eleven, and left with seven captives including Britt's pregnant wife, Mary, and their two children, Jube and Cherry.

During the winter, Britt Johnson sent inquiries to ac-quaintances in Indian Territory and learned the probable whereabouts of his family—the High Plains of the Panhan-dle. In the spring, he rode for the High Plains.

Britt did not find his family right away, but he ransomed other captives he found and returned them to their grateful kin in Young and Montague counties. On his third trip into hostile territory, he finally found his own brood. Some accounts say the U.S. Army helped Britt regain his family. Others say Britt's friend Comanche Chief Asa Havey (Milky Way) helped him recover his wife and children.

Britt himself told how he found the band holding his loved ones and convinced them that he was tired of white men and wanted to become a Comanche. He demonstrated his strength and marksmanship, and the Comanches accepted him and reunited him with his family. After several months, Britt and his family—including an infant born among the Indians—escaped. They moved farther east to Parker County.

Britt had gained almost legendary status among whites for his ability to track Indians and deal with them. But the Indians regarded him as a traitor. Britt and two other black men were freighting supplies near old Fort Belknap on January 12, 1871, when twenty-five Kiowas attacked.

The three teamsters killed their horses and used the carcasses as breastworks, but the Indians soon killed Britt's two partners. Though he used three rifles to hold off repeated charges by the Kiowas, the Indians finally killed Britt, scalped him, and mutilated his body. A burial detail found 173 empty shell casings around Britt Johnson's body. He died violently, but with the stripe of heroism that had elevated him from slave to legend.

COWBOY SAILOR

A cowboy had to make a living somehow, and Charles Siringo, for one, "hated the idea of being busted." After he got fired from his first job herding longhorns up the trail to Kansas, he spent his last dollar getting home to Tres Palacios and had to find some kind of work.

Charlie met a factory hand with a boat for sale for forty dollars. Siringo had grown up on Tres Palacios Bay and could handle a sailboat as well as a cow pony. The factory worker agreed to trade the boat for a horse as long as it wasn't "Ol' Satan"—Siringo's horse. "No one would have him as a gift," Siringo explained.

A fellow named Horace Yeamans had a nice-looking horse he wanted to get rid of. No one wanted the animal, however, because it always became lame in both front legs after trotting just a short while. Siringo knew that, but the boat owner didn't.

Siringo traded his interest in three different brands of cattle for the crippled horse and fourteen dollars. Yeamans later "sold the cattle for enough to buy a whole herd of crippled ponies."

Charlie gave the crippled mount and ten dollars in return for the boat. The horse soon went lame on its new owner, as Siringo knew it would. "Such is life in the far west," he lamented.

Siringo named his boat *The Blood Hound* and plied the waters of Matagorda Bay throughout the summer of 1875, loaded with melons, oysters, or passengers. In October he decided to get his boat into the Colorado River and "speculate among the Africans that lined the river banks."

The mouth of the Colorado had always been plugged by a massive raft of driftwood, preventing boats from entering. Siringo would have to move his craft overland five miles from the head of Wilson's Creek to the head of the raft to get into the Colorado.

Loaded with tobacco, "snide jewelry," and "tanglefoot," Siringo sailed up Wilson's Creek with a new partner called "Big Jack." The partners expected to trade their goods for "hides, pecans, etc.," which they could have shipped to Indianola.

With rollers under *The Blood Hound*, Siringo and company pulled the boat onto the prairie with oxen. About that time, Big Jack got into the tanglefoot, got drunk, and ran off with the merchandise, which he sold at a loss to whomever would buy.

Charlie Siringo was stuck with an empty sailboat sitting on dry land and a crooked partner selling his goods all the way back down Wilson's Creek. He sold *The Blood Hound* where she lay for twenty-five dollars, hunted up Ol' Satan who was running loose on the range somewhere, and went "back to my favorite occupation, that of a wild and wooly cowboy."

Siringo spent fifteen years as a cowboy, three years as a merchant, and twenty-two years as a Pinkerton detective agent. He wrote about his adventures in several books. His most famous book carries an interesting subtitle which revealed his familiarity with sailing as well as cow punching. It is called *A Texas Cowboy—or—Fifteen Years on the Hurricane Deck of a Spanish Pony*.

HILL COUNTRY HERMIT

He was a Texas Hill Country hermit from 1836 to 1862.
He survived by hunting deer, black bear, wild turkey, and
other abundant game species. He befriended Indians, lived
in a cave, and was buried there. His name, according to legend, was Adolf von Verthein.

But did he really exist? You'll have to draw your own
conclusions on this one; the story of "The Hermit of the
Cavern" is one of the oddest and most mysterious tales in
the folklore of Texas.

The best place to start explaining this story is in 1876.
That year, a German-born Texan named August Siemering
wrote a German-language novel entitled *Ein Verstehltes
Leben*—"A Wasted Life." The plot seemed too strange and
melodramatic to be true, but Siemering noted that he had
based his story on actual events in Texas.

The novelist's bittersweet story line revolves around the
tragic life of a character named Adolf von Verthein. As the
story begins, Adolf is a fiery young lieutenant in the
German army, 1835. One night he sees his best friend apparently flirting with his sweetheart. Enraged, Adolf
challenges his friend to a duel. The friend's only honorable
course is to accept. They fight the duel, and Adolf inflicts a
severe wound on his friend. As the loser lies bleeding, he
explains to Adolf that his conversation with the girlfriend
had been purely innocent.

Overcome with guilt and shame, Adolf immediately
quits the country and breaks all ties with family and friends.
He boards a ship to New Orleans, finds his way to Texas,
becomes a wanderer and a recluse. He throws in with a band

of Lipan Apaches who show him to a secluded Hill Country cave where he makes his home.

It might have been a great adventure, hunting the Texas Hill Country before the onslaught of civilization. But Adolf is tormented by the death of his friend and the loss of his sweetheart. Once in a great while he longs for human company and ventures from his cave to make the rounds among a few acquaintances in the Hill Country—mostly German immigrants.

In 1862 the old recluse dies a hero, mortally wounded while rescuing a friend from one of the novel's villains. On his death bed he makes a tragic discovery. As he reveals his identity to ask that someone notify his family in Germany of his death, he learns that one of the young men attending him is his nephew, sent to Texas to look for him. The nephew explains that the friend Adolph had wounded in the duel in Germany had completely recovered long ago and forgiven the entire affair. Adolf's sweetheart had never married, but had moved in with Adolf's sister to await some word from the wanderer.

Had Adolf not fled from his troubles in Germany with such haste, things could have turned out quite differently. The hermit of the cavern dies at his nephew's side, knowing now that he has truly lived a wasted life. At Adolf's request, his German-Texan friends bury him with his guns and few possessions in the nameless cavern he called home.

So much for fiction. After the first printing, the novel disappeared from public scrutiny for over fifty years. Then in 1932 a University of Texas professor, May E. Francis, found a copy of *Ein Verstehltes Leben* and decided to translate it and revive it under the title *The Hermit of the Cavern*. Here's where the story takes yet another strange twist.

That same year, 1932, Cascade Caverns were discovered near the old German settlement of Boerne. Plans were made to turn the spectacular cavern into a tourist attraction. Coincidentally, the translator of the novel and the developer of the cave met, compared notes, and found that the description of the cave in the novel matched the actual appearance of the newly discovered cavern near Boerne.

During development of Cascade Caverns, Lipan Apache arrowheads were found. Then, while excavating silt and dirt from the cave floor, workers found a human skeleton and a corroded revolver of antebellum vintage.

The German-Texan novelist August Siemering once lived only fifteen miles from the place where Cascade Caverns would later be "discovered." Did the tragic character Adolf von Verthein really exist? If so, Siemering certainly used a fictitious name, so no means of tracing the hermit back to Germany exists.

How close to reality was the story of Adolf's wasted life? It is a Texas mystery that may never be solved.

THREE-LEGGED WILLIE

Judge Robert McAlpine Williamson, better known as "Three-Legged Willie," held his first term of court at Shelbyville where the Regulator-Moderator War had stirred things up in East Texas. Neither faction intended to let the Republic of Texas take charge of things in the area. They had plans to prevent Judge Willie from holding court.

When Judge Williamson called the court to order, a representative came forward and presented Willie with a resolution to dismiss the first case up for trial. Willie wanted to know by what law or authority. The local representative drew a long Bowie knife from a belted scabbard and placed it on the table in front of the judge. "This is the law in this country," he said.

Three-Legged Willie produced a Colt pistol from his holster and placed it on top of the knife saying, "This is the constitution that overrules your law." The court convened on schedule.

As a frontier judge, Robert M. Williamson served the Republic with alacrity despite his obvious physical handicap. A childhood disease had left Willie's right leg permanently bent at the knee. He walked on a wooden leg strapped to the afflicted knee. Williamson had special trousers made that covered both his real right leg and the wooden addition which gave him the appearance of having three legs.

As a member of the Texas Legislature, Three-Legged Willie once expressed his opposition to a certain piece of legislation by announcing, "I go against this bill with both my arms and all three of my legs!"

Despite his adventurous spirit and his robust service to Texas from the San Jacinto battlefield to the floor of the legislature, Judge Williamson reportedly suffered frequent bouts with an illness of a very peculiar order. According to Campbell Wood, a contemporary of Willie's, the judge had spells of paralysis during which he could neither move nor speak but remained aware of everything going on around him.

While in this strange state on the second floor of an Austin hotel, Williamson's nurse mistook him for dead. The carpenters came around and measured Willie for a coffin. The judge remained unable to move or speak as they brought the finished product for him to try on for size. Luckily, the woodworkers had forgotten to account for Willie's bent leg and his right knee stuck up over the top of the coffin. The carpenters had to take it away to make the sides higher.

The second time they came around, Judge Willie called upon all his faculties to protest as they lowered him into the box. He kicked with all three legs and cursed with sudden vigor. When the "corpse" showed signs of life, the carpenters dropped everything and bolted for the door. The nurse jumped from a second-story window and somehow escaped injury.

Judge Three-Legged Willie escaped an even more dangerous drop of some six feet.

NICKNAMING THE WEST

James B. Miller was a stalwart of the Methodist Church in Texas around the turn of the century. Business was steady with Miller, but he frequently took time off from work to preach at camp meetings and prayer services. He could deliver a sermon with such ardor that his acquaintances came to know him as "Deacon Jim" Miller.

Like any good western nickname, "Deacon Jim" Miller possesses a certain agreeable cadence. It trips easily across the tongue. It emphasizes an interesting facet of the owner. It is authentic, and by no means contrived, for in the frontier West, sobriquets were as common as tracks around a water hole.

A singular talent or peculiarity in behavior led to many a nickname in the old days. Charlie Siringo, author of the classic *A Texas Cow Boy*, was so adept at knife throwing that he frequently used his blade to kill rattlesnakes from the saddle on the ranges of Texas and New Mexico. His unimpressed cowboy friends dubbed him "Dull Knife." When he quit punching cattle and went to work as an operative for the Pinkerton Detective Agency, Siringo occasionally used "Dull Knife" as a cover name.

Often a single incident could warrant a moniker that would stick. A California horse thief named Jack Allen once wore an iron vest to make his line of work a little less dangerous. He survived four barrels of buckshot and became popularly known as "Sheet Iron" Jack.

Bodily characteristics often resulted in epithets, and westerners never pretended not to notice a physical abnormality. Arizona had "Three-Fingered" Jack Dunlap,

Colorado produced "Cockeyed" Frank Loving, and "Wild" Bill Hickock's murderer, John McCall, was known as "Broken Nose Jack." Also on the subject of broken noses, a horse thief named George Curry once got kicked in the face by some stolen property and thereafter answered to "Flat Nose" Curry.

An old shotgun wound gave notoriety to New Mexican bounty hunter Andrew "Buckshot" Roberts. Similarly, a near miss led to the rechristening of Charles Bryant, a train robber from Kansas. Bryant was once fired upon with a pistol at close range. The bullet only grazed his cheek, but the permanent marks left by the powder burns gave him the name of "Black-Faced" Charlie.

The Texian Aylett C. Buckner, who stood six-foot-six and weighed 250, was known everywhere as "Strap" Buckner for his strapping physique.

Trail driver A.H. Pierce, the most successful cattleman on the coastal bend of Texas, went by the name of "Shanghai" because he walked with the cocky strut of a Shanghai rooster.

Noah Smithwick lived in Texas from 1827 to 1861 and mentioned quite a few Texas nicknames in his book *Evolution of a State* (1900) and in an article specifically about nicknames in volume 2 of the 1898 *Southwestern Historical Quarterly*. During Texas' colonial days, wrote Smithwick, "domestic animals were so scarce that the possession of any considerable number gave notoriety and name to the possessor." Thus "Cow" Cooper, "Hog" Mitchell, and "Sheep" Brown earned their handles.

One of the first colonists to settle where the town of Brazoria now stands planted popcorn on his claim, Smithwick recorded. The field became known as the popcorn patch. Later, another settler bought the land, and though he never raised popcorn, he became known as William "Popcorn" Robinson.

A picayune was a Spanish coin that gave its name to "Picayune" Smith, who ran a store in Victoria. "Waco" Brown survived an "enforced sojourn" among the Waco Indians. "Gentleman" Bob Williams exuded an impression of gentility among buckskinned frontiersmen because he wore store-bought clothes. "Pot" Williams once smashed a cooking vessel over an adversary's head during a mild altercation. "Dog" Brown allegedly appropriated another man's canine. A mill blade mangled "Sawmill" Cooper. "Ramrod" Johnson had perfect posture, and "Varmint" Williams captured live animals for menageries back East.

Smithwick's contemporary, Erasmus "Deaf" Smith, really was hard of hearing, but he performed miracles of espionage as Sam Houston's chief spy during the Texas Revolution. His nickname is affixed permanently on the map of the Texas Panhandle across Deaf Smith County.

The origin of William A. "Bigfoot" Wallace's nickname, wrote Smithwick, is uncertain. Aside from his fame as an Indian fighter, soldier, and frontiersman, Bigfoot was known as a master raconteur. He seems to have spun several yarns about how he won his appellation.

Certain groups of men seemed to spawn epithets with more prolificacy than others. The Texas Rangers had Ernest "Diamond Dick" St. Leon who wore expensive jewelry, and Matthew "Old Paint" Caldwell whose strange white-splotched complexion reminded his contemporaries of a paint horse. Ranger John "Rip" Ford earned his appellation as an army adjutant during the war with Mexico. One of his duties involved sending death notices to the families of American casualties. Such grim missives usually included the words "Rest In Peace" or at least "R.I.P."

Buffalo hunters claimed handles almost to a man. "Smokey Hill" Thompson hailed from the Smokey Hill River in Kansas. "Snakehead" Thompson sold whiskey among the hunters and, knowing they liked libations of a venomous variety, sank a few rattler heads in each barrel of whiskey he sold. "Dirty-Faced" Jones simply never washed his face.

Perusal of Wayne Gard's formidable work *The Great Buffalo Hunt* (1959) yields nicknames such as "Squirrel-Eye" Emory, "Moccasin" Jim Stell, "Limpy" Jim Smith, "Whiskey" Jim Greathouse, "Spotted" Jack Dean, "Hurricane" Lee Grimes, "Buckskin" Bill Godey, "Windy" Bill Russell, "Prairie Dog" Dave Morrow, and "Wild Skillet."

In *I'll Tell You a Tale* (1931), J. Frank Dobie recorded how Mayberry Gray earned his nickname. Hunting buffalo far from camp one day, Gray was knocked from his horse by a mortally wounded bull. His horse ran off with the bison herd. Gray made a lariat of twisted bison hide, perched on a tree limb near a water hole, and lassoed a mustang stallion coming to drink. He then made a rawhide hackamore and, riding bareback on the wild stud, returned to camp after several days' absence. He was known thereafter as "Mustang" Gray and was immortalized by the ballad of the same name.

Then there was a certain hide hunter by the name of Jones. One day the right rear wheel of Jones' wagon broke down. Some other hunters came along and told him that an abandoned wagon just like his sat eight miles away. He endeavored to find it and retrieve a replacement wheel from it. When Jones returned a few hours later without a wheel, he told his companions that only the left rear wheel of the abandoned wagon was sound, and that was the wrong wheel. His friends burst into laughter and explained to Jones that all the wheels were interchangeable. The embarrassed buffalo hunter was ever after renowned as "Wrong-Wheel" Jones.

As for women on the frontier, nicknames seemed common only among sporting girls. James N. Browning, a lawyer and politician from Mobeetie, Texas, recorded a story about "sporting soubrequets" (sic) in the *Panhandle-Plains Historical Review* (V.32, pp. 95-100):

"The grand jury indicted all the courtesans of the town, under their various sporting soubrequets, given to them by the cowboys and gamblers, many of which names were rare and racy."

Browning did not take the liberty of listing the sporting names, but he said the judge, while calling the docket, became so embarrassed that he was moved to remark, "These courtesans do have the queerest names I ever heard in my life!"

"Big Nose Kate" was a barroom girl who met "Doc" Holliday in Texas, helped him escape a lynch mob, and became his common-law wife. Doc, of course, derived his nickname from his doctorate in dentistry. He belonged to an elite corps of lawmen, outlaws, and gamblers who became known as gunfighters and spawned sobriquets with admirable celerity. Bill O'Neal, in his remarkably useful and readable volume *Encyclopedia of Western Gun-Fighters* (1979), recognizes this tendency and explains many nicknames.

"Gunfighters. . ." O'Neal writes, ". . .were so liberally labeled with appellations that many of them are hardly known by their real names. . ."

"Mysterious" Dave Mather was a gunman who liked to maintain a shadowy profile. The gambler John O'Rourke went by the handle of "Johnny-Behind-the-Deuce." Frederick "Dash" Wait and Nathaniel "Zip" Wyatt possibly earned their monikers by virtue of fast shooting.

Oklahoma's Doolin-Dalton gangs included outlaws such as "Red Buck" George Weightman, "Tulsa" Jack Blake, and the explosives expert "Dynamite" Dick Clifton. Another gang member so frequently sang the cowboy ditty "I'm a wild wolf from Bitter Creek," that he became known as George "Bitter Creek" Newcomb. "Arkansas" Tom Jones was really Roy Daugherty of Missouri whose nickname and alias were intended to cover his trail.

Some westerners even managed to earn more than one nickname. Will Christian was known as "Black Jack" because of his dark complexion and "202" because of his weight. Then there was William Brooks who was known variously as "Buffalo Bill" or "Bully" Brooks.

The category of multiple nicknames brings us back to James B. Miller, that stalwart of the Methodist Church in Texas, otherwise known as "Deacon Jim."

You see, Jim Miller claimed a second epithet—a rather incongruous one at that. Nobody knows exactly how many men Miller killed. "I have lost my notch stick on Mexicans," he once bragged. People had a habit of turning up dead around Jim, starting with his grandparents, in 1874, when Jim was only eight. (He was arrested but never prosecuted.) At seventeen, Miller shot his brother-in-law dead, then went on to a varied outlaw career. He is suspected of murdering Pat Garret in 1908. He was lynched in 1909 with the three men who hired him to murder (successfully) Oklahoma rancher Gus Bobbitt.

So it appears that when "Deacon Jim" wasn't preaching impromptu sermons at camp meetings, he answered to the handle of Jim "Killer" Miller. He would murder just about anybody for a hundred and fifty dollars.

THE DRAWBACKS OF FIRE HUNTING

In his own time, Robert Hall's name evoked the same awe in Texas as the names of Davy Crockett or Bigfoot Wallace. For some reason we seem to have forgotten him today.

Hall was a Texas soldier, pioneer, Indian fighter, hunter, and scout. As a hunter, Hall knew few equals. He owned a carved powder horn, given to him by Sam Houston, which once belonged to the pirate Jean Lafitte. In old age he wore a coat which he stitched together himself from the hides of animals killed in Texas. A biography, *Life of Robert Hall*, published when Hall was eighty-five, describes the garment:

"The coat is composed of over 100 different pieces. A piece from the hide of every wild beast and from many reptiles and birds finds a place in the curious and attractive garment. Of course, skins of deer, bears, panthers, wolves, and wildcats make up the larger part, but a connoisseur in such matters would readily find pieces from a hundred other animals. The coat is trimmed, or rather ornamented, with the hoofs of 315 deer, the claws of forty bears, the tails of innumerable smaller animals, and the rattles from hundreds of monster rattlesnakes."

Hall undoubtably shot many of the critters that made up his coat by firelight in the dead of night. Fire hunting was popular in those days. Hunters either carried a torch or a lantern or built a big bonfire and waited until they saw eyes glowing in the dark, then started blasting away.

In addition to all his other talents, Robert Hall was a practiced raconteur. One of his favorite campfire tales describes a fire hunt where the darkness and the excitement of the hunt became too much for even the fearless Robert Hall.

Hall went out that night with a fire lamp and "an old smooth-bore, flint-lock musket that carried forty buck-shot." He soon started shining the eyes of "the big game" and took a shot at the largest set of fire-lighted eyeballs he had ever seen.

"I am not clear as to the occurrence of this world for the next few moments," said Hall. First he thought a boiler had bursted, then he figured a cyclone had passed over him. Finally he realized that the old smooth-bore musket had knocked him senseless. "I was lying on the ground and the old musket was still quivering." Fearing that the "young cannon" would kick him again, Hall struck it with a club.

"I was lying some 10 or 12 steps from where I was standing when I pulled the trigger and several trees were bent and twisted between me and my original position." The fire hunter managed to stand up, but then he could hear the musket cocking itself and sharpening its flint. He started running and tripped over "one of the biggest old bucks that was ever killed in Texas." He thought he heard the gun coming after him, ran a few more steps, and tripped over a second buck in the line of fire.

"I had no idea what I had not killed," said Hall. "I feared that some of the shot might have gone on over the hill and killed some of my stock, or perhaps my wife and children." Inspired by a sudden burst of courage, Hall crawled back to the musket. He snuck around to the "safe side of it"—the muzzle—and held the dangerous butt away from him. Then he tied the demoniacal musket to a tree with his suspenders and went home to brag about killing two big bucks with one shot. "The wonder is that I did not kill more."

Back in the horse and buggy days, a couple of South Texas hunters drove their one-horse buggy into the chaparral for a night hunt with a lantern. They left the buggy and wandered around in the mesquite until they realized they were lost. Then they saw two eyes glowing in their lantern light. Judging from the distance between the eyes and their height above the ground, the hunters knew they must be looking at a huge whitetail buck. One shot dropped the animal in its tracks—not to mention its buggy harnesses. The hunters had to walk home.

Some time back in the 1840s a young fellow from Vermont named Gabe Calvin decided to try hunting deer by firelight over a man-made deer-lick. You see, Gabe had talked himself into a tight spot. He had raved and boasted about the amount of game he had bagged back in "Old Varmount," but he had yet to pull a trigger in his new home. He became anxious to prove himself.

So Gabe made a deer-lick in a likely looking spot by drilling an old log full of holes and filling the holes with salt. A week later Gabe told everyone in the settlements that his deer-lick had attracted—as he could tell from the hoof prints thereabouts—a two-year-old buck.

Gabe didn't own a gun, so he persuaded his employer, an old farmer, to let him borrow an ancient "Queen Anne's piece, long as a liberty pole, with a bore you could stick your fist in." He filled the old musket "about half full of powder and buckshot and slugs and such destructives." Gabe made a torch by whittling a piece of wood until it bristled with shavings. Then he repaired to a blind overlooking his deer-lick at about sundown.

In time, Gabe heard the distinct crack of a dry twig at a distance through the woods. His heart pounded like a pile driver. The faint sounds of his quarry's hooves trodding the forest floor came nearer, and finally Gabe heard the gnawing of wood and knew that his two-year-old buck stood just yards away in the dark at the deer-lick.

Cautiously, Gabe lit his match and touched the flame to his torch. As the wood shavings flared, he saw the glare of two eyes, aimed in their general direction, and let the old musket roar. Buckshot and slugs went one way as Gabe went the other, propelled down the slope and into the muddy pool by the recoil of the rifle.

When Gabe returned to the cabin, dazed and muddy, he hung the old musket back on its pegs and went straight to bed, refusing to address any questions. The next morning he barely bore a resemblance to his former self. His cheek was so swollen that only one eye would open. His shoulder was one tremendous bruise.

He had hit his target, though—put twenty holes clean through it, as a matter of fact. But his "two-year-old" turned out to be a yearling, for the next evening one of the farmer's heifers didn't come home. Gabe Calvin soon had plans to head back to "Old Varmount."

PART 2

WILD TIMES

SAN FELIPE CURSE

Despite Stephen F. Austin's attempts to populate his colony with only the most respectable citizenry, immigrants of tarnished reputations also filtered in. U.S. Army deserters, counterfeiters, murderers, and other miscreants came to Texas to escape various jurisdictions.

Noah Smithwick came to Texas in a youthful search for adventure and became a blacksmith at the colonial capital of San Felipe. The suspicious characters, wrote Smithwick in his book *Evolution of a State*, were ones such as himself who denied any criminal activity abroad when asked what trouble had caused their flight to Texas. Any fugitive who admitted his former indiscretions fit right in.

Smithwick remembered a few lines from a poem about San Felipe that caused a local bard to acquire a new suit of tar and feathers despite the veracity of his verse:

> *The United States, as we understand*
> *Took sick and did vomit the dregs of the land*
> *Her murderers, bankrupts, and rogues, you may see*
> *All congregated in San Felipe*

Of course, Smithwick's forced departure from the colonial center did little to swell his heart with fondness for Old San Felipe.

The town had no jail, so when a friend of Smithwick's allegedly committed a murder, he was put in chains with little hope of a speedy trial. Smithwick slipped his friend a file and a pistol. The suspect escaped but lingered in the nearby woods where authorities tracked him down and killed him. In his possession they found Noah Smithwick's gun.

The colonial authorities found Smithwick guilty of aiding the felon in a "Star Chamber" proceeding which he wasn't invited to attend. The first notice Smithwick received of the charge against him came from a squad of militiamen who arrived one day to carry out the sentence— immediate banishment from Texas. "Considering the character of the place, it was about the best thing they had ever done for me," the blacksmith would write later.

As his escort put Smithwick on a horse, some San Felipean ran into the street with a bottle and a glass and suggested that Smithwick propose a toast to Old San Felipe. Smithwick raised the glass and, before draining it, said, "If there is an honest man in the place may he be conducted to a place of safety, and then may fire and brimstone be rained upon the iniquitous town."

Five years later, in 1836, Old San Felipe indeed burned to the ground to prevent Mexican troops from looting it after the fall of the Alamo. Smithwick liked to believe his curse had something to do with San Felipe's fiery fate.

FAITH HEALER

In the 1880s, the U.S. Postal Service sent an investigator to South Texas. The post office at Los Olmos, north of present Falfurrias, showed a peculiar discrepancy between the large number of correspondence sent there, and the small amount of postage sold there.

The fault was with Don Pedro Jaramillo, faith healer. Thousands of ailing individuals from as far away as New York wrote to him regularly, asking for remedies to their ills. Most of them could not afford to pay, but almost all of them included return postage with their letters.

The *curandero* had come to Los Olmos Ranch in 1881 from Mexico where, he said, God had given him the gift of healing. At first he traveled from his *jacal*, making rounds to Corpus Christi, San Antonio, and Laredo, helping the sick cure themselves through their own faith. Soon, however, such a constant procession of patients lined up at his door and camped around his hut that he had to stay at home most of the time.

Thousands of Mexicans and Anglos, Catholics and Protestants came to him for cures. "Don Pedrito" always knew at a glance what ailed them. A single patient might also describe the maladies of several friends too weak to travel. Jaramillo would send his prescriptions for each with the visitor.

The healer never asked for payment from his patients, but those who were able paid in currency or goods—perhaps a horsehair rope or a live chicken. Jaramillo gave much of the money and goods he received to his poorer patients. He always dressed and lived as a common laborer.

The remedies of Don Pedro Jaramillo often followed common sense. A man came to him with a grass burr caught in his throat. Jaramillo made him drink salt water until he threw up, dislodging the burr. Don Pedro told a hypochondriac who complained of migraines that her head must be cut off and thrown to the hogs if the condition continued. The headaches went away. Jaramillo told a doubter faking an illness to eat a bale of hay.

Other patients received more arbitrary prescriptions:

Drink a glass of lukewarm water nine successive mornings, first saying, "In the name of God."

For one day, wear shoes filled with canned tomatoes.

For nine nights in a row, under the stars, take a drink of water from a glass and pour the remainder on the ground.

Wear the same clothes for nine days, soaking them nightly with water and sleeping in them.

He did not claim to have a cure for everyone. When one man made a long journey to see Jaramillo, the healer offered no remedy, but he told the man God would cure all his ills before he reached home. The traveler died on the road.

Don Pedro Jaramillo died in 1907, but his miracles still work today. Believers still make pilgrimages to his simple tomb, one mile east of Falfurrias on Texas 285, and three miles north on Farm Road 1418. Candles burn around the clock. Abandoned crutches and letters from cured ones give lingering testimony to the power of Don Pedro Jaramillo's faith as a healer.

HOME REMEDIES

Not all frontier Texans who claimed perfect health really enjoyed it. Some just lied about their ills to get out of taking home remedies which were often worse than the ailments they were meant to treat.

If you had asthma, for example, you might not want to admit it just so you could avoid taking the remedy of kerosene mixed with the grease from a fried skunk.

For tuberculosis one treatment involved burying the afflicted victim up to the neck in goat manure for a morning—a very long morning.

Arthritis sufferers would sometimes boil an old shoe and drink the water. Cures for the common cold included boiling an armadillo shell and drinking the brew. For rheumatism, the therapy was to boil a buzzard, extract the grease, and rub it all over the patient's body.

Most Texans avoided getting earaches at any cost lest they should wind up with one of the following remedies in their ears: warm chicken fat, the melted grub of a dirt dobber, a drop of June bug blood, a cockroach boiled in oil.

No wonder some Texans preferred other remedies like four quarts of hard cider to purify the blood; hot ginger, sugar, and whiskey for a cold; whiskey and quinine for chills.

Along coastal areas, malaria constantly ailed many residents with chills and fever. Liqour was the common folk remedy, and Wharton County rancher J.D. Hudgins was as folksy as anyone when it came to therapeutic drinking.

In fact, the Hudgins family and the family doctor, "Coon" Davidson, talked J.D. into checking himself into a Fort Worth hospital noted for treating alcoholics. Dr.

Davidson, though he had a total hearing loss, was a devoted family physician and accompanied J.D. Hudgins from Wharton to Fort Worth on the train.

Apparently, Hudgins began to have misgivings about his impending treatment on the way to Fort Worth. When he and the doctor arrived, they met two hospital attendants with a buggy at the depot. What J.D. Hudgins said to the two attendants went something like this:

"Gentlemen, I am Dr. 'Coon' Davidson of Wharton and this old fellow," indicating the real Dr. Davidson, "is my patient, J.D. Hudgins. He's not wholly reconciled to the prospect of institutionalization for his alcoholism, so he's sure to raise sand when you put him in your buggy. But be firm and take him anyway."

The real Dr. Davidson couldn't hear a word of the conversation, of course, but conceived the gist of it when the two hospital attendants forced him aboard the buggy under duress. J.D. Hudgins caught the first train back to Wharton County.

Eventually, things worked out. "Coon" Davidson managed to establish his true identity and secure his release from the hospital, and J.D. Hudgins learned to use more sensible remedies than alcohol for fever and chills—like cow chip tea.

THE GREAT HANGING

Civil War hysteria hit Gainesville harder than any other Texas town in October 1862. A secret plot to overthrow the Confederacy surfaced. Chaos reigned, bullets flew, hanging ropes uncoiled. In the final tally, at least forty-four men had died.

A secret "Peace Party" had been recruiting members in Cooke County. Ostensibly, its goal was to peacefully restore the Union. Under these pretenses, as many as 1,700 Union sympathizers joined. They took oaths of loyalty and learned the secret sign, password, and handshake of the "Order."

But as recruits got deeper into the Peace Party, they were expected to take part in a planned raid on Confederate ammunition supplies. Any recruit who tried to back out had his life threatened. Some of them later claimed that any man, woman, or child unfamiliar with the secret sign, password, and handshake would have been killed had the Order come to power.

The Confederate army got wind of the covert clan and sent in a spy who got a long list of names. On October 1, Confederate soldiers and Cooke County militia units began making arrests. Throngs of soldiers, militiamen, prisoners, civilians, and "screaming women and children" pressed toward Gainesville. The sixty-eight captured members of the Order were held in a "strong prison home." There was talk of hanging every prisoner immediately.

A public meeting was called that day. A committee was appointed which selected a jury of twelve men. This "citizens' court" of dubious authority was to decide the fate of each prisoner by majority vote.

The first seven men tried were sentenced to die and were hanged from an elm tree on October 4. At this point, some of the more moderate jury members threatened to quit the citizens' court if the automatic hangings didn't stop. A chord of moderation resulted, and most men from then on were released or held until they could be turned over to military authorities.

When the death sentences stopped, however, the mob in the streets of Gainesville became so thirsty for blood that it broke an accused horse thief out of the local jail and lynched him. The mob then threatened to storm the prison and execute every man at once unless twenty more were sentenced to hang. The citizens court negotiated, and reluctantly consented to condemn fourteen more men to the gallows to prevent a general massacre.

The jury adjourned for a week to let the mob fervor cool. But during that week, some still-at-large members of the Order murdered two Confederate men along the Red River, and the angry mob assembled again outside the prison. Of some forty-five prisoners still being guarded, the citizens' court sentenced nineteen more to hang. The others were finally released.

After about three weeks of utter madness, forty members of the Order had died by the rope, two had been shot trying to escape, and two Confederate men had been shot.

After the war, some members of the so-called citizens' court went on trial themselves for their part in the hangings. They were acquitted, but the "Great Hanging" haunted Gainesville, Texas, for decades after the war.

FRONTIER SURVEYORS

A party of ten surveyors rode west from Bastrop in 1838 to locate lands. Within a day or two, one of them, an old man of the frontier, returned. He said he deserted when the younger men on the surveying team refused to post guards around their camp. The old-timer predicted Comanches would massacre the entire party.

When the surveyors failed to return, a search party rode west and found the skeletons of nine men. Several bee trees had distracted them from their surveying chores. They were chopping down the trees to rob them of honey when the Indians attacked. One mortally wounded surveyor, left for dead by the Comanches, had carved his name on a felled bee tree as his final deed.

The very nature of the frontier surveyor's job thrust him into the strongholds of hostile tribes. Indians learned quickly that men carrying transits and chains represented harbingers of further white encroachment into their hunting grounds. Comanches called the surveyor's compass "the thing that steals the land."

Surveyors who went unarmed tempted fate. A party of land locators in Calhoun County, 1834, neglected to take guns with them. When they spotted Karankawas skulking into position for an attack through tall grass, the unarmed surveyors used their wits in lieu of weapons. They shouldered sticks as they would rifles. At the tailgate of their ox cart, they disguised a camp kettle to look like the muzzle of a cannon swinging into position to fire. The "Kronks" fell for the deception and retreated.

Surveyors and Indians clashed time and again on the Texas frontiers. In the "Surveyor's Fight" of 1838, twenty-some-odd land locators battled an entire day with some 300 Kickapoos. Only seven white men survived.

Josiah Wilbarger, Texas' legendary survivor of the Comanche scalping knife, lost his hair while locating lands for new colonists. Even the original surveyors of the capitol grounds in Austin could only work safely under guard of Texas Rangers in 1839.

In Indian country, surveyors did their work hastily, often locating only two or three corners of each tract instead of going all the way around the boundary. This caused inaccuracies and overlapping claims which later led to land feuds.

When Indians couldn't kill the surveyors, they destroyed notes, stole equipment, and bashed compasses.

U.S. Army Capt. Randolf B. Marcy explored vast tracts of Texas with compass and telescope between 1849 and 1854. Friendly Indians acted as his guides, including a famed Delaware scout named John Bushman. Bushman's tracking abilities made him an archenemy of hostile Comanche bands.

One night Marcy trained his instruments on the heavens to figure his distance from the Canadian River. He reckoned his party would find the river the next day, but Bushman claimed the Canadian lay much farther to the north. When the party reached the river the next day, as Marcy had predicted, the Delaware scout was awed.

"Captain," John Bushman was quoted as saying, "look at stars again, and tell me where Comanches gone."

CHAMPS D'ASILE

The hunting has been pretty good in southeast Texas in recent times, with open seasons on deer, squirrel, doves, quail, waterfowl, and even pheasant. Over 175 years ago, however, the hunting was so good in that region that it may have changed the course of world history!

The story begins with Napoleon's defeat at Waterloo in 1815. After almost three decades of warring in and around Europe, the emperor surrendered to the British and was forced into exile on Britain's remote St. Helena Island, 1,200 miles off the west coast of Africa.

Many of Napoleon's followers, however, escaped the British and came to America. Among them were General Charles Lallemand, Lieutenant General Antoine Rigaud, and Napoleon's brother, Joseph Bonapart, whom Napoleon had made king of Spain from 1808 to 1813.

In early 1818, General Rigaud landed on Galveston Island with 150 men, 600 muskets, 400 sabers, and 1,200 pounds of gun powder. A couple of months later, General Lallemand arrived on the island with more troops. Jean Lafitte, the privateer of French heritage, guided the Napoleonic generals to Galveston and offered to help them.

Galveston belonged to Spain in 1818, and Spain prohibited settlement of Texas by foreigners. But the Frenchmen had little respect for the edicts of Spain. Jean Lafitte had been using Galveston as a pirate base for about a year, in defiance of the Spaniards. Napoleon's generals cared even less about Spain's claim to Texas. They had been at war with Spain for ten years.

In boats purchased from Jean Lafitte, the Frenchmen sailed across Galveston Bay to the mouth of the Trinity River. From there, most of the troops proceeded on foot, while a few oarsmen rowed upstream with the supplies toward the chosen site of a settlement to be called Champs d'Asile. The colony was located on the Trinity River somewhere near present-day Liberty. The boats, which carried most of the provisions, became lost in uncharted tributaries, and the men on foot went hungry for several days.

When the boats and provisions finally arrived, the Old Guard began building four forts and several log cabins at Champs d'Asile. Rations were short—a biscuit a day one soldier wrote.

When Champs d'Asile was in place, General Lallemand issued a decree to the world describing his settlement as a peaceful, agricultural colony with laws founded on "justice, friendship, and disinterestedness." But the Napoleonic leaders were not as disinterested as they would have the world believe. Their real mission in Texas was to instigate the Mexican Revolution for Independence, situate Joseph Bonapart in Mexico City as "King of Spain and the Indies," and plan the rescue of Napoleon from St. Helena Island.

It might even have worked if the Frenchmen hadn't gotten sidetracked. The woods in the Trinity bottoms were crawling with game in those days. Deer, turkey, black bear, game birds, and small game animals abounded. Wolves, coyotes, foxes, mountain lions, and bobcats provided additional sport. Probably the only hunting the aristocratic generals had engaged in before coming to Texas was of the European variety where game was scarce. To them, Texas was a hunter's paradise.

These French military men were no frontiersmen. They did not prove efficient enough as hunters to feed an entire army. The hunting was obviously a recreation reserved for a few officers. The regular soldiers spent most of their time bivouacking or building cabins. As a result, food supplies shrank.

"An army travels on its stomach," Napoleon is supposed to have said. It is ironic, then, that his generals allowed their men to starve in the fertile Texas wilderness, while they enjoyed the many diversions of sport hunting.

After about five months, Indian messengers arrived at Champs d'Asile with word of a Spanish military force on its way to expel the Frenchmen. The French troops were so starved, and their morale so low, that General Lallemand decided to abandon Champs d'Asile and flee to Galveston.

A hurricane struck the island about the time the Frenchmen arrived and ruined what few provisions they had left. The men mutinied. Chaos ruled. "Thefts, brawls, duels and assassinations" occurred.

The Old Guard scattered. Some crossed the bay and walked to Alexandria or Nachitoches, Louisiana. Some joined Lafitte's corsairs. Some sailed to New Orleans on a ship that Lafitte gave them to get rid of them under pressure from Spain and the U.S.

In the end, "about half . . . perished either on the island or in Texas, from disease, overwork, hunger, misery, duels, and assassinations; two others had been taken and eaten by the hordes of savages (Karankawas) who sometimes land at Galveston."

The outcome might have been different if Lallemand and Rigaud had recruited a few experienced Indian or American hunters to feed their army. The forces at Champs d'Asile might have fended off a Spanish attack if they had been well fed. Such a victory might have hastened Mexican Independence. Mexico was ripe for revolution anyway and gained independence from Spain in 1821, just three years after Champs d'Asile.

If the Frenchmen had caused the revolution to start earlier, and if they had taken part in it, they could have then used Mexico as a base to plan Napoleon's rescue from St.

Helena. Napoleon died on St. Helena in 1821, but some historians have suggested that he might have lived much
longer if he had been given proper medical attention.

Napoleon was only forty-nine the year of Champs
d'Asile. If the great emperor had been freed, nursed back to
health, and brought to Mexico, there's no telling how the
history of Texas and the world might have been changed. He
might even have lived long enough to do battle with William
B. Travis at the Alamo, or Sam Houston at San Jacinto. He
would have been sixty-seven that year.

But, as it turned out, generals Rigaud and Lallemand
got sidetracked sport-hunting the abundant southeast
Texas wildlife while their army went hungry. Champs
d'Asile met its waterloo, a relatively inconsequential and
almost forgotten page of Texas history.

INDIVISIBLE

Texas is big now, but imagine the size of her as a republic. Back then the Panhandle had a panhandle. The western Texas border followed the Rio Grande to its headwaters and beyond, into what is now Wyoming.

Some said Texas was too big. Her size made her difficult to govern from one capital. Divergent religions, cultures, economies, and traditions—not to mention weather and geography and Indians—made taking a pair of scissors to the Texas map sound like a good idea to many parties.

That's why Texas entered the Union in 1845 with the right to divide into as many as five states. Almost from that moment, division plans went into action—and for some good reasons. Divided into five states, the same area would have ten votes in the U.S. Senate instead of two. Each state would also have its own governor and state congress to deal with regional issues.

In 1850 Texas sold a big chunk of territory to the U.S. and shrunk by one-third to its present size. But that was still too big for the divisionists.

In 1852 came a plan to divide Texas along the Brazos.

In 1857 a group of abolitionists in Boston wanted to organize southwest Texas into a non-slave state.

Reconstruction disunity caused further plans for division. A segregationist wanted an all-black territory in west Texas, and the U.S. Congress came up with a three-state division idea in 1868.

Another proposal would have lumped El Paso County together with southern New Mexico to create the "Territory of Montezuma."

In 1869 a group of divisionists wrote and published a constitution for a proposed "State of West Texas." It would have encompassed everything southwest of the Colorado and east of the mouth of the Pecos. Since wild varmints outnumbered the constituency there, opponents called it the "State of Coyote."

The divisionists took their fight to Washington and had congressmen from other states propose bills to divide Texas into multiple states or territories such as the "State of Lincoln."

In 1871 came the first plan to tear Texas into four states.

A West Texas legislator in 1891 suggested that East Texas join the state of Arkansas.

One unique plan in 1906 called for dividing Texas into four states which would share a governor but have their own legislatures and their own representatives in Washington.

The "State of Jefferson" was proposed in 1915 to encompass 117 West Texas counties.

U.S. Congressman John Nance Garner (who would later become vice president) in 1930 threatened to break Texas into five states to give the South greater representation in Congress.

Even as late as 1938, a group mentioned the possibility of creating a state from three South Texas counties.

How did Texas remain intact? Anti-divisionists in Texas politics managed to kill or defeat all proposals or bills that would have rent the state asunder. They had only one good reason for opposing division. As stated by the *Memphis News*, "the people of Texas, so long as there is a drop of the Alamo blood in their veins, will resent to their last breath the division of Texas or the excision of a foot of, to them, hallowed territory."

THE GREAT CADDO LAKE PEARL RUSH

Caddo Lake, on the Texas/Louisiana line, has a catfish tradition older than any other lake in the state. Since the earliest days of settlement, the favorite traditional catfish bait at Caddo was the freshwater mussel. Countless mussels lived in the many shallows that existed along the lake's shores back then, and collecting them was a simple matter of wading.

Pearls in freshwater mussels are rare, but Caddo Lake seemed to have an uncommon wealth of them. It was not unusual for a fisherman to turn up a pearl while shelling a mussel for bait. Pearls form around any foreign substance that irritates the tender flesh of the mussel. A grain of sand or a parasite might cause the growth. It has been suggested that the Caddo Lake mussels were plagued by some prolific parasite that made pearls more common there.

In the early days, the lucky pearl finder usually gave the gem to his sweetheart. But in 1909 a Japanese immigrant with an obscure past thrust Caddo Lake into a pearl boom!

George Sachihiko Murata's past was a mystery to residents in the Caddo Lake area; he wouldn't talk about it. Rumor suggested that his head was wanted on the emperor's chopping block for some reason back on his native island. Caddo Lake folks would soon find out, however, that he knew a thing or two about pearls.

Murata worked as a cook at an oil rig on the Louisiana side of Caddo Lake in 1909. One day that summer Murata was looking for bait to use in catching a catfish dinner for the roughnecks and roustabouts of the oil rig. He pried open a freshwater mussel from the shallows of Caddo Lake and found a pearl within.

The find was not unique, of course, but George Murata, unlike the other Caddo Lake residents, somehow had a knowledge of the commercial value of his find. He sold it to a pearl buyer for $1,500. That far exceeded the average annual salary of an oil field cook in 1909. A few days after his first discovery, Murata found another pearl of equal worth.

Murata wasn't greedy. He didn't try to keep the pearl resource a secret. He let the word of its value get out, and the great Caddo Lake pearl rush began.

Farm families converged on the moss-shaded lake from all quarters. They set up a tent community at Potter's Point, on the Texas side, and launched a combination lake-party/treasure-hunt that would last for three glorious summers.

The men and boys waded for mussels while women and girls kept camp or opened the shells. The "pearl hogs" waded barefoot in the vast shallow flats of Caddo Lake. When they felt a mussel with their feet, they would grasp it with their toes, or dive for it, and then open it to check for pearls. Some hunters towed small wooden boats around by a rope tied to their waists. They would toss the mussels into the boat to be opened later on shore.

Pearl hunting provided a welcome change of livelihood for the hard working farmers. Their fields could survive the lack of tending in the summer, and the cool waters of Caddo Lake invited them with promises of hidden riches. Families regarded their pearl hunts as vacations—profitable ones, at that.

Many farmers made only $300-$600 a year from their crops. With luck, they could match that with a single pearl find. Most pearls sold for $20 or $25, but exceptional specimens brought as much as $100, $500, even $900. A typical run of luck could produce $50-$75 of pearls a day. But no one ever topped George Murata's two early pearl sales of $1,500 each.

The hunters turned pearling into a science. They knew which types of mussel would produce which kinds of pearl. A large, flat-shelled variety known as a "washboard" mussel yielded the most valuable pearls. A pink pearl came from the "white-eyed" mussel, and a wine-colored gem came from the "buttermilk" mussel.

Buyers came from Arkansas where freshwater pearls were already being marketed. Of course, not every mussel contained a gem, but when a hunter found one, he shouted out, "Pearl!" Then the buyers rushed to him in boats to appraise the pearl on the spot. Sometimes the hunter held an impromptu auction, taking bids while standing chest deep in water.

As long as warm weather facilitated wading, the pearl hunting continued. The pearlers came back in the summer of 1910 and again in 1911. Commercial catfish fishermen of Caddo Lake virtually abandoned catfishing for pearling. As many as a thousand fortune seekers might be seen wading the mussel beds at times.

As quickly as it began, the bonanza came to an end. And wouldn't you know the government would have a hand in the demise of Caddo's pearl industry. A new government dam went in near Mooringsport, Louisiana, which caused the lake level to rise. The mussel beds became too deep to wade. Methods of obtaining the shellfish with dredges and other equipment proved unprofitable.

George Murata had found only two pearls during the entire rush, but then he only hunted mussels for fish bait. When catfish once again became the lake's favorite crop, he stayed on at Caddo and opened a fishing camp on the Texas side where he died in 1946. His past remained a mystery, and no one ever found out the origin of his secret knowledge of pearls.

MUTINY ON THE *SAN ANTONIO*

Sergeant Seymour Oswald of the Republic of Texas Marine Corps was not only a conniving, murdering mutineer, he was a lucky rascal. In 1842 Oswald was Sergeant of Marines aboard the Texas navy's war schooner *San Antonio*.

On the night of February 11, the *San Antonio* was anchored at New Orleans where her high-ranking officers were engaged in cavorting about the town. The crew and Oswald's company of marines, however, were confined to quarters. A few bottles of smuggled liqour did nothing to improve the temperaments of the confined men. Oswald and some other disgruntled sailors decided to see about improving their situation.

On deck, Oswald could suddenly be heard asking a lieutenant for shore leave. The young officer refused to grant the privilege, and an argument ensued. Charles Fuller, the ranking officer on board at the time, appeared atop decks and the shouting accelerated. Then Fuller made a big mistake. He ordered the marines to take arms and uphold his authority even though the sergeant of the marines was the main instigator of the unrest.

Oswald's marines armed themselves and led an attack on the officers. Fuller died, and two other officers received wounds. The band of mutineers then lowered boats and fled. It was a reckless, ill-advised move by Seymour Oswald, but he couldn't have better improved his chances for longevity had he been clairvoyant.

Within a few days, New Orleans police had the mutineers locked up in the city jail. They could not be released, however, until President Sam Houston arranged for extradition. So, while Oswald and his band awaited extradition and court martial, the *San Antonio* sailed for Yucatan.

In September 1842, the accused mutineers got a lucky break. The *San Antonio* went down somewhere off the coast of Yucatan taking its entire crew—including many witnesses to the mutiny—to a briny grave. The mutineers, too, would have gone down with the ship had they not revolted in New Orleans.

Extradition finally came through in April of 1843—over a year after the mutiny. New Orleans turned the prisoners over to the Texas navy for court martial at sea. The prosecution would have had difficulty proving guilt without any living witnesses to testify against the accused men. But one of the mutineers, Frederick Shepard, turned state's evidence in exchange for a pardon. Shepard told the court that a mutiny had been planned for months before it occurred. The mutineers originally wanted to capture the *San Antonio* and sell it to Mexico, he said.

Frederick Shepard received his pardon but died three weeks later in a naval battle with Mexican vessels. One of the accused mutineers had died in jail at New Orleans. Three received lashes with a cat-o'-nine-tails, and four others were hanged from the yard arms of the Texas navy sloop-of-war *Austin*.

The only mutineer to escape justice was the murderous, conniving, but lucky, Seymour Oswald, the leader of the mutiny. He had escaped from jail in New Orleans and was never heard from again.

COTTON BALES

"If all the bales of cotton grown in Texas could be made into one stack, you would have a stairway reaching the pearly gates," says an old Texas brag. Indeed, cotton appears with such regularity in Texas history that the standard unit of trade for the crop—the bale—has come to some rather unusual uses.

Before the Civil War, the U.S. Army imported several camels for experimentation in the arid West. The camels landed at Indianola and marched west to Camp Verde, sixty miles northwest of San Antonio, where they became permanently stationed.

On the trip westward, the "Camel Brigade" soldiers used cotton bales to construct temporary enclosures for the camels. Apparently, the camels carried the bales with them. Each camel could carry two bales. At each camp along the way, the soldiers arranged the bales into a temporary corral.

Pauline Shirkey Clark told of seeing the cotton bale pens, as quoted in Chris Emmett's book *Texas Camel Tales*: "The bales of cotton had been used for a sort of pen to keep them (the camels) from straying . . . While we were there . . . a fight occurred between the camels. O! They were ferocious! Major Wayne cried out: 'Get back; get back on the cotton bales'. . ."

As the *Monitor* and the *Merimac* made Civil War history in their famous battle of the ironclads, few historians took note of the Confederacy's "Cottonclads" of Matagorda Bay. Captain E.S. Rugeley of the Confederate navy needed some protection for his ships' gunners. He used bales of cotton to build improvised bulwarks on the decks of his ships. Because of their density, the cotton bales served as bulky yet effective shields around the gunners.

A historical marker on the south side of the Matagorda County courthouse in Bay City explains how the crewmen of the Cottonclads had a more difficult time with waves than with bullets. A sudden norther swamped the fleet's skiffs and drowned twenty-two men engaged in a nighttime attack on a Union beachhead.

Though the cotton bulwarks in Matagorda Bay were not able to save drowning persons, cotton bales served precisely that purpose twelve years later in Indianola. When the devastating hurricane of 1876 hit that port city, tides swelled more than fifteen feet above normal levels. Residents clung to any bouyant objects to escape the high winds and water. Some enterprising survivors lashed bales of cotton into rafts and managed to float to safety miles inland.

So the cotton bale—that lasting boon to the Texas economy—has spared many a Texan not only from unemployment, but from flood waters, enemy bullets, and even ferocious camels. Reaching the pearly gates is another matter.

TEXAS TREES

A 1922 U.S. geodetic survey determined the precise geographical center of the state of Texas near the town of Mercury. On that very spot stands a famous tree: the Heart O' Texas Oak. Many loyal Texans regard this oak as the axis around which revolves the universe.

Many other Texas trees deserve distinction for their places in history rather than geography. Comanches, on their annual treks south, liked to camp along Hamilton Creek where it now flows through Burnet. To mark the spot, they bent a live oak sapling to the ground and tied it there. Today the Indian Marker Tree retains its horizontal posture, but Comanches no longer pass.

Near San Saba, the Matrimonial Oak served as an altar for Indian weddings. Settlers later continued the legendary tradition by swapping vows under the same branches.

Tradition says a youngster, Martin Flemming, climbed an oak tree one night in 1854 to escape Indians. Years later, the town of Comanche grew up around the oak. The town grew so much over the years that it decided to chop the old oak down to facilitate paving the town's public square. When workmen arrived with axes, they found a grim old-timer there with a shotgun in his hands. "Uncle Mart" Flemming said that as long as he drew breath, no axe blade would touch the tree that saved him as a boy. His tree—the Flemming Oak—stands today on the town square of Comanche, Texas.

Other Texas trees mark the triumphs and tragedies of war. In 1842 fifteen La Grange men volunteered to join the fight against an invading Mexican force. They gathered under the Muster Oak. In decades to come, young men would muster beneath the same branches for service in the war with Mexico, the Civil War, the Spanish-American War, and both World Wars.

On the river in San Antonio, the Ben Milam Cypress stands near the point where its heroic namesake died. Milam led a force of about 300 Texans to a six-day battle in the 1835 ousting of Mexican troops from San Antonio. A Mexican sniper shot and killed Milam from the boughs of this cypress during the fight.

Another Texas hero, Sam Houston, left a tree at nearly every turn of his illustrious career. In 1847 Houston pulled up a pecan sapling to use as a buggy whip. Once home in Huntsville, he planted the switch in his yard and it became the Houston Pecan.

In 1849 Houston campaigned for public office under a live oak in Marshall and used the same shade in 1857. The tree became known as the Houston Campaign Oak. Also in the 1857 campaign, at San Marcos, Houston kissed a number of young ladies who had sewn a Texas flag for him. An overshadowing oak was dubbed the Kissing Oak.

In the more desperate days of his career, a week after Alamo, General Houston began his retreat from Gonzales known as the Runaway Scrape. A huge live oak called by that same name still stands ten miles east of Gonzales where the Texian army camped for the first night of the retreat.

Thirty-four days later, Houston's army, still retreating, came to a crossroads. The Which-Way Oak remains rooted at the same crossroads today, eight miles east of Tomball. The left road led to Nacogdoches, continued flight to Louisiana, and maybe the end of the Republic. The right fork led to Harrisburg, the San Jacinto River, and a certain clash with Santa Anna. The destiny of Texas depended on Sam Houston's command of "column left" or "column right" in passing that tree.

Sam chose the right path.

THE NATIVE PECAN

The pecan tree is one of Texas' few native plants that produces a substantial cash crop every year. From earliest times Texas residents have relied on the annual yield of the beautiful pecan tree.

Early explorers and settlers commented on the delicious nuts and noted that many wildlife species utilized them, including turkeys, black bears, and, of course, squirrels. Most of the native trees had small nuts with thick, hard shells. But a few exceptional trees bore extraordinary pecans, and those individual trees determined the future for the Texas pecan industry.

E.E. Risien had probably never even heard of a pecan when he left England in the early 1880s to come to Texas. He settled in San Saba, started a family, and developed and operated the town water works.

The pecan was not a big cash crop in those days, but the tasty nuts were collected from the native trees and sometimes sold at the trading square. Risien took a particular liking to them.

One of Risien's children dropped some pecan nuts near the water works and they sprouted readily. Perhaps because he had worked as a cabinet maker, Risien took an interest in cultivating pecan trees and planted a row of them along the road into town. San Saba residents snickered at this crazy foreigner who spent his time planting trees that already grew wild by the hundreds along the river.

As Risien studied pecans he began to take note of different varieties. Some trees, which he termed "mother trees," produced superior nuts. He learned how to graft branches from the mother trees onto year-old seedlings grown in five-gallon cans. When Risien began selling his improved trees, San Saba residents quit snickering.

One day someone brought Risien a bag of particularly fine pecans. The pecan expert put a nut between his teeth to crack the shell. To his surprise, the shell yielded like paper. Risien called the variety "papershell deluxe" and bought seven bushels at five cents a pound. Then he sold them to nurserymen across the country at one dollar a pound.

Risien found out that the papershell mother tree stood at the confluence of the San Saba and Colorado rivers, nine miles from town, on a piece of land considered public property since the owner lived in Alabama. When requests began to arrive from nurserymen who wanted limbs from the mother tree to use in grafting, Risien went to inspect the tree. To his horror, he found that the seven bushels he had bought had been harvested by sawing every limb but one from the mother tree. The remaining limb was spared only because the fellow who had sawed off the rest of the limbs had used that one to stand on.

Risien bought "the best piece of pecan land in the state" from the Alabama owner and began to nurse the original papershell pecan tree back to health. He moved his family onto his 320-acre triangle of land and began farming, grafting, pollinating, and planting pecan trees. "I muddled through somehow with a little bunch of cattle, horses, turkeys, chickens, pigs, and fish, squirrels, and pecans," said Risien in a 1927 interview. "This is in brief how I came to be a pecan crank."

Risien became the world's foremost expert on Texas' state tree. He sent papershell pecans to Queen Victoria. The "lord high steward, royal palace dietician" corresponded with Risien about the nuts.

The San Saba Mother Pecan still stands. It is the source for some of the most famous varieties of pecans in the industry, including Liberty Bond, Jersey, No. 60, San Saba Improved, Texas Prolific, and Western Schley.

In 1900 a couple of boys, brothers named Burkett, were hunting squirrels along Battle Fish Creek in eastern Callahan County. Apparently, one of them killed a squirrel in its nest and had to climb up and retrieve it, because along with their dead squirrels the boys brought home a cache of pecans they had found in the nest. When their father, J.H. Burkett, saw the unusually fine pecans, he sent the boys right back into the creek bottoms with orders to find the mother tree from which those pecans came.

After a prolonged search, the brothers located the tree. J.H. Burkett tried for three years to graft limbs from the mother tree onto other pecans and finally succeeded in 1903. In 1910 the original mother tree was destroyed, but by that time, Burkett had firmly established his variety of papershell pecans which were particularly suited to the sandy soil of the Cross Timbers region.

Another famous tree that still stands is the Jumbo Hollis Pecan near the little town of Bend on the Colorado River in San Saba County. The first owner of the tree was an early settler named Thomas I. Hollis. He couldn't help noticing that his tree produced huge pecans. It usually took seventy to eighty native pecan nuts to weigh a pound but an average of just thirty-three of Hollis' pecans tipped the scales at that weight.

The Jumbo Hollis variety won a bronze metal at the 1904 World's Fair in St. Louis and even made it into Robert L. Ripley's "Believe It or Not" column. Around the turn of the century many grafts were made from the Jumbo tree, establishing the Jumbo Hollis as a commercial variety. In 1919 this one tree produced half a ton of pecans by itself. The tree was worth a small fortune because its nuts sold for as much as a dollar a pound.

The native Texas pecan tree is good for all sorts of things. Its wood is among the hardest of all hardwoods and is used in cabinet making. Its nuts are among the tastiest of any nut-bearing tree in the world. Its spreading boughs give much needed protection from the blistering Texas sun.

Some anthropologists theorize that the pecan tree may have extended its range from the lower Mississippi River valley into Texas with the help of prehistoric Indians who traded for them and planted them here. Like Sam Houston, Stephen F. Austin, and Bigfoot Wallace, the pecan may not have started out Texan, but it got here as soon as it could.

THE COLORADO RAFT

The Colorado, second-largest river within the borders of
Texas, contributed relatively little to the state's transportation needs. Even though some of the earliest Texas settlers
lived along the lower Colorado, the river proved virtually
useless as a navigational route because of a raft of driftwood
blocking its mouth.

Alonso de Leon first reported the raft in 1690. It remained and grew over the next 150 years as seasonal floods
washed debris downstream. In some places, the raft floated
on the surface of the river, letting the current slip through
underneath. In other spots, waterlogged timber jammed
right into the river bed. Some of Santa Anna's retreating
soldiers may have crossed it on foot after San Jacinto.

Flatboats could ply the river above the raft. They drifted
down with the current and had to be poled or sailed upstream. But early Texans wanted to open the Colorado to
steamboats entering from the Gulf of Mexico, so in 1837 the
Congress of the Republic of Texas created the Colorado
Navigation Company (CNC) with headquarters in
Matagorda, at the river's mouth. The company had four
years to clear the raft using toll money levied on steamboats
and other vessels in Texas. Four years later the raft
remained.

In 1844 Congress rechartered the CNC and built a
steamboat above the raft. The *Kate Ward*, a 115-foot side-
wheeler with a draft of only eighteen inches, chugged into
Austin in 1846 amid wild fanfare. She could carry 800 bales
of cotton but could only work the river from Austin to the
raft. From there, goods were hauled overland to Matagorda.

During a flood in 1848, the *Kate Ward* slipped around the raft on high water, which proved to be a mistake, because afterwards she couldn't get back in.

The technology existed by then to remove the raft. But Texans just couldn't raise the $40,000 to $80,000 estimated for the task.

In 1851 Texas again reactivated the impotent CNC which converted the *Kate Ward* into a "snag boat" equipped with steam powered saws and winches. At a cost of $17,000, she cleared the river twenty miles above the mouth, but the raft still extended another twenty miles upstream. This was the closest the CNC ever came to removing the Colorado raft.

In 1854 the U.S. Corps of Engineers finished digging a canal around the raft, and steamers could at last traffic the Colorado. Five steamers and dozens of flatboats hauled pine timber and cotton out to the gulf. The Colorado was still treacherously shallow. Only steamers that could "float on a heavy dew" traversed her. The steamer *Colorado* struck bottom below La Grange and sank.

Union engineers withdrew from Confederate Texas during the Civil War, and driftwood filled the canal around the raft. The Colorado's short era of navigability ended. By 1871 railroads had reached Austin, and interest in navigating the Colorado waned.

The debris collecting around the raft caused flooding in Wharton and Bay City. In 1929 a canal was cut along the eastern edge of the raft, allowing the river current to carry away the jammed timber. That year a flood swept almost the entire mass of debris into the Gulf.

After hundreds of years, the raft was finally no more.

SOLID RANGE

The state of Texas claims a public lands history unique in the United States. Most states entered the union as territories, but Texas joined the U.S. as an independent republic. When Texas became a state in 1845, it retained its unsettled public lands instead of ceding them to the federal government. The state managed to legally retain this possession of public lands even through secession and reconstruction.

Over the following decades, the state granted or sold its public lands to railroads, universities, ranchers, and homesteaders until virtually all range in the state had fallen into private hands.

The land began to run out around the turn of the century. By then, only school lands remained unclaimed. Since the days of the Republic, Texas had set aside public school lands to lease to stock raisers. The lease revenue went toward education.

In much of northwest Texas, school land made up every alternate section. Many private ranches were checkered with sections of public land which they leased every year. Those ranchers wanted to own those sections so they could have "solid range."

But in 1895 a new state law allowed settlers to file on school land, live on it three years, and thereby earn ownership. Nesters could file on one section for farming or four sections for grazing. A wild land scramble began and lasted almost a decade before all school lands had fallen into private hands.

During this time, the occupation of "bonus-hunter" arose. Bonus-hunters were opportunists who filed on available lands, then sold their contracts to other parties at a profit or "bonus." Some of them made profits of three dollars an acre. Once they sold their claims, the bonus hunters were free to file on other sections.

But bonus-hunters were not the only opportunists who manipulated the land laws. Many families used the names of their minor children or far away relatives to file on sections. Some "land pirates" even filed claims on behalf of their dogs.

Other settlers were really cattle rustlers who wanted to own property surrounded by ranches with cattle they could steal.

But the large ranchers didn't intend to stand by while land grabbers took up every other section of their grazing land. When nesters filed on sections within their pastures, the ranchers used every method they could devise to gain possession of the land and make their range solid.

Some ranchers traded with the nesters. A shrewd settler could trade his surrounded section for perhaps two or three sections on the edge of the ranch.

Other ranchers encouraged "friendly nesters" to settle, then leased the land from them. The friendly nester could live on his land and be employed by the ranch. The rancher let the nester collect his lease in merchandise through an account at the ranch store. Often, the nester became so indebted to the store that he had to sell his land to the ranch.

Other ranchers had their cowboys file on school land within their spreads. The cowboys built shacks in which they supposedly lived. At the end of three years, the cowhands turned their new deeds over to their employers.

Many sections of former school land changed hands time after time before the big pasture men finally got control. Drouths forced many of the nesters to sell, and in the end, the ranchers usually won their solid range, but not without cost.

THE PLAN OF SAN DIEGO

The factors that drew the United States into the first World War were global in scope. However, some South Texans may suggest, even to this day, that the deciding factor had its beginnings in the town of San Diego.

In 1915 five years of revolution had plunged Mexico into anarchy. The revolution also took on an increasingly anti-American stance. Texans along the lower Rio Grande Valley began to get nervous.

In February, thousands of handbills circulated across South Texas inciting Mexican nationals and Americans of Mexican descent to rise up against Anglos from Texas to California and reclaim all former Mexican territories.

No one yet knew whose ambitious mind had concocted the visionary scheme, only that it had been drafted in San Diego, Texas. Thus the plot became known as the Plan of San Diego.

The uprising began slowly—almost unnoticeable. A few raids and holdups occurred, but were thought the mischief of the normal criminal element. Throughout the summer of 1915 the raids grew more frequent and became clearly the work of bandits striking from south of the border. The marauding bandits burned bridges, derailed trains, killed travelers, and stole livestock.

Citizens asked the U.S. Army for help. Several Army units were garrisoned in the Valley, but claimed the raiders were Texans and that state and local authorities should deal with them. Texas lawmen and vigilantes engaged the raiders in several shootouts, lynched some suspects, and shot others who were "trying to escape."

Still, the raids continued almost daily, and sniping from south of the Rio Grande also became a problem. Especially for U.S. soldiers still forbidden to return fire.

Some fifty miles north of the border, a large raiding party met a posse of lawmen on a part of the King Ranch. The Texans killed twenty-three raiders and found several German Mauser rifles left on the battlefield. On at least two other occasions, raiders questioned whites about their ancestry and took care not to molest those of German descent. In a nighttime battle near Mission, Americans killed seven raiders including a Japanese agent.

The raids and sniping continued to the point where some Texans began sleeping in their cornfields to avoid attacks on their homes. Finally the U.S. Army authorized retaliation and moved several more units of cavalry, infantry, and artillery into Brownsville, Harlingen, and Del Rio. The border raids began to die out, especially after General Pershing chased Pancho Villa across the border for raiding a New Mexico town.

By then, intelligence sources had intercepted messages from German secret agents. Germany wanted to help Mexico achieve the Plan of San Diego with additional aid from Japan. The Kaiser wanted the U.S. in the war, and Americans obliged him.

TEXAS SANITARIUM

Consumption and other lung disorders caused incalculable suffering in Texas and elsewhere before the days of modern medicine. However, in an indirect way, such diseases actually contributed to things like Texas independence, industry, law and order, and literary recognition.

Doctors advised victims with persistent coughs and breathing problems to seek warmer, drier climates. Many chose Texas as their sanitarium. Erastus "Deaf" Smith left a family plantation in Mississippi and came to San Antonio in 1821 because he had consumption. He hunted and ranched in Texas and claimed wild game—particularly skunk meat—improved his constitution.

Smith was Sam Houston's best spy during the Texas Revolution. He intercepted invaluable intelligence which helped Houston plan for battle. He went disguised into enemy camps. At San Jacinto the daring spy destroyed "Vince's Bridge," preventing Santa Anna's escape. Deaf Smith's disease caught up with him about a year after San Jacinto. He died at the age of fifty.

Gail Borden sought the warmer climate of Texas in 1822 to rid himself of a debilitating cough. He served the Texas Revolution as editor of *The Telegraph and Texas Register*, a dangerous job considering Santa Anna's views on freedom of the press. He became wealthy and successful years later in the milk business and contributed to Texas industry.

The family of sixteen-year-old Leander H. McNelly moved to Texas from Virginia in 1860, hoping to better his consumptive condition. A year later he enlisted in the Confederate army, became a captain at age nineteen, and led a company of guerrilla scouts. After the war, L.H. McNelly commanded the legendary Special Ranger Force of the Texas Rangers. He battled hundreds of rustlers between the Nueces and Rio Grande with his thirty men.

But the frail 135-pound McNelly spent much of his ranger career bedridden. He tried goat milk to improve his health. Once, when he went home to recuperate, his wife converted a wagon into a camper so he wouldn't have to sleep outside while in the field. His medical bills represented one-third of his ranger company's expenses. McNelly died of consumption at age thirty-three in 1877.

William Sidney Porter came to Texas to shake a hacking cough and later achieved fame as O. Henry, the short story writer. His story "A Fog in Santone" described the large community of consumptives living in San Antonio in the 1880s.

C.W. Post came to the Panhandle in poor health in 1886. He left as the healthy, multimillionaire leader of the Post Cereal Company and the founder of Post, Texas.

Doc Holliday added color to Texas history if nothing else. He was a Georgia dentist until his consumption drove away his patients. He rode on to immortality in Arizona's O.K. Corral.

Thousands of ailing individuals came to Texas simply for the climate. Texas gave them hope of recovery or longer life. Many of them repaid her in ways too varied to recount.

"COME AND TAKE IT"

Those who frequent gun shows usually go looking for a bargain or a particular piece to round out a collection. But when Dr. Pat Wagner of Shiner went to a San Antonio gun show in 1979, he turned up what is in all likelihood an artifact from one of the most pivotal moments in Texas history.

The centerpiece of the 1979 Texas Gun Collectors Association Gun Show in San Antonio was an old iron cannon identified as a Spanish piece from the period 1820-1835. When Dr. Wagner saw the little cannon on display and read a card saying that it had been "unearthed in Gonzales," a recollection came to mind.

"My daddy had always told me that Mexicans and Texans fought over a cannon in Gonzales," he said. "He told me that story every time we went through there."

The cannon was then owned by Mexican rancher and gun collector Henry Guerra. It was badly pitted by corrosion and weighed only sixty-two pounds, but was built stout with one-inch-thick iron comprising the barrel. "It had no trunnions on the sides," Wagner says, "but it had a ball on the back end and about a ten-gauge bore."

Bobby Vance, president of the Texas Gun Collectors Association, liked the piece so much that he acquired it from Guerra. Later, Dr. Wagner acquired it from Vance and began looking into its history. Wagner found out that the cannon had been discovered in Sandy Creek, between Gonzales and San Antonio, by a fellow named Lowell Cooper in a 1936 flood. "He was fishin' bodies out when he found it," Wagner says. Cooper hauled the rusted old cannon out of the creek, put it beside some nearby mailboxes, and went on searching for the bodies of flood victims.

A rural mail carrier found the cannon at the mail boxes and took it to the Gonzales post office where it remained for many years. Later, the gun was moved to the home of a Gonzales postmaster. Members of the postmaster's family eventually took it to a Houston gun show where Henry Guerra purchased it and took it to Mexico.

Once he had learned all he could about the history of his cannon, Wagner began looking into the story his father had told him about the cannon that Mexicans and Texans had fought over in Gonzales, hoping to find some link between his cannon and the Gonzales cannon.

Many Texas history books mentioned the fight. It happened in 1835, when American colonists in Texas were beginning to talk about war with Mexico. The Mexican government had given the town of Gonzales a small cannon to use in scaring away Indians. But now Santa Anna wanted the cannon back to prevent the Texans from using it against the Mexican army.

Some Mexican cavalrymen rode to Gonzales to take the cannon, but the Texans refused to give it up. They loaded the cannon with scrap iron, designed a flag that included a depiction of the cannon and the words "Come And Take It," and attacked the Mexicans at dawn, October 2, 1835. Though the scrap metal fired from the Come and Take It Cannon didn't draw any blood, the blast has long been recognized as the first shot in the Texas Revolution.

Unfortunately, about the only detail Dr. Wagner could find about the cannon itself said that it had been brass, and his piece was iron. Undaunted, he continued to study the relic, not really sure what he was looking for.

Since retired, Wagner was at the time a practicing physician and treated his cannon much like a patient. He put a mirror down the muzzle, trying to examine the inside of the barrel "like an ear, nose, and throat doctor." He also X-rayed the cannon in the clinic at Shiner but only got a picture of the outline.

It wasn't until Wagner tried a medical fiber optic scope that he began making new finds. Inserting the scope down the muzzle, he was able to see evidence that the cannon had once been worked on near the breech. Then an industrial radiologist at the San Antonio airport figured out a way to X-ray the cannon from the inside out, and he found "a flared bushing about the size of a man's thumb" near the breech.

Still, it wasn't until a friend brought an old book to Wagner's attention that the pieces of the puzzle started to fit. The book, *Evolution of a State*, was written by Noah Smithwick, a Texas pioneer who arrived in Gonzales the day after the Come and Take It Cannon fired the first shot in the Texas Revolution.

Wagner was elated to read Smithwick's description of the Gonzales cannon as "an iron six-pounder." Being an expert gunsmith, Smithwick would have known the difference between iron and brass. He worked on the cannon in a Gonzales blacksmith shop to get it into better shooting order. He wrote that the cannon had been "spiked, and the spike driven out, leaving a touch-hole the size of a man's thumb."

This means that someone had driven a spike into the original touch-hole of the cannon to make it virtually useless as an effective artillery piece as it could only be fired by means of a fuse run down the muzzle. Then the spike had been driven back out, probably by the Texans, leaving an enlarged touch-hole. Wagner believes Smithwick closed or narrowed the enlarged touch-hole with a bushing like the one the X-rays had revealed in his cannon.

But Smithwick's book lends even more evidence supporting Wagner's claim that his gun is very likely the original Come and Take It Cannon. Smithwick said he and his helpers mounted the cannon on some old wooden wheels with a wooden axle, dubbed it "the flying artillery," hitched two yokes of longhorn steers to pull it, and set out with the Texas volunteers to take San Antonio.

But the wooden wheels soon began to smoke on their axle. The Texans tried water and tallow to ease the friction, but the flying artillery had to be "abandoned in disgrace at Sandy Creek before we got halfway to San Antonio." Sandy Creek is, of course, the name of the place where Dr. Wagner's cannon appeared in the 1936 flood, a hundred years after the Texas Revolution.

Dr. Wagner has since received letters from the Smithsonian Institution, the Texas State Archives, and various military historians and metallurgists stating that his cannon could very well be the old Come and Take It Cannon from Gonzales. The gun is on display at the Gonzales Memorial Museum, except when Dr. Wagner takes it on the road for special events.

He still refers to himself as a "jack-leg gun collector" and visits gun shows, but he will probably never top finding the cannon that fired the first shot in the Texas Revolution.

THE CANEBRAKES

Imagine a wall, seventy miles long, twenty to twenty-five feet high, from four to forty miles thick. When the American colonists came to Texas, such a wall existed between the lower Brazos and Colorado rivers, along the course of Old Caney Creek.

The natural wall consisted of a native cane or bamboo, the stalks growing so close together that a person could scarcely squeeze through. Vines and briars intertwined among the stalks, binding the cane poles into a formidable barrier.

Karankawa Indians used the cane to make arrow shafts with which they hunted and shot fish. They also made cane fish traps from the stalks. When settlers moved in, they found an inexhaustible supply of fishing poles in the canebrake. Fastened together, the cane stalks made flooring or matting. Picketed in rows they became light fencing. Their chambers filled with tallow created crude candles. The young, green shoots served as feed for livestock.

In 1836 John C. Duval came to fight in the Texas Revolution. Captured with Fannin's men, Duval made a miraculous escape from the Goliad massacre and began an arduous trek northward to find Houston's army. He progressed relatively well until he reached the canebrake.

He searched for a road leading through the brake but only found lobo wolves, panthers, black bears, turkey, deer, wild hogs, and mustangs. All the American colonists along the southern fringes of the canebrake had fled, fearing the approach of the Mexican army. Duval decided to cut his own path through the canebrake with a carving knife he had taken from an abandoned cabin. "I therefore attacked the cane, green briars, and bushes with a carving knife, and after working faithfully till late in the day, I found I had gone about three hundred yards."

When he came to a large tree in the brake, Duval climbed it to see how much more cane he would have to cut. "I could see an ocean of cane," he said, "at least four miles in the direction I wished to go, and beyond the scope of vision to the northwest and southeast."

Dejected, Duval collapsed at the bottom of a tree outside the canebrake. He fell asleep. Scout, a stray dog he had picked up at the abandoned cabin, woke him up barking. A big black bear was coming down the tree. Duval leaped clear as the bear hit the ground and crashed through the canebrake, popping the stalks like a runaway wagon.

Duval continued to search for a road through the brake, using his inherited cabin as a base camp. He found many deer trails that led into the cane, but they soon gave out or weaved around aimlessly. For five days he searched the flanks of the cane forest for a path, occasionally hiding from small parties of Mexican soldiers and Indians.

A herd of six or seven hundred mustangs galloped by the canebrake one day. At night Duval heard the howl of lobo wolves and the screams of panthers around his camps. Scout wanted to chase one lion near the campfire, but Duval "declined hunting panthers in the night with a carving knife." On another occasion, however, he fought a bobcat for a chicken.

Camping out one night, Duval heard "a great many turkeys" flying up to roost all around him. Their gobbling woke him in the morning. He found several hundred turkeys perched within fifty yards of his bedroll. Without a gun, Duval couldn't take advantage of the game, and the turkeys seemed to know it. He had to throw a stick at one fat gobbler to make him fly.

Almost ready to give up, Duval decided to take a closer look around the cabin he kept returning to for supplies. He found a hidden road just a few hundred yards from the cabin. It seems the settlers had expected war with Mexico for some time and had carefully concealed the entrances to their escape routes through the canebrake.

It was sunset when Duval walked half a mile into the canebrake to make sure he had indeed found a road. The cane stalks reached high above the narrow road, drooped inward and intermingled at the top, creating a tunnel-like appearance. The Texian soldier decided to stay one last night at his cabin and march through the cane in the morning.

On the way back to the cabin, however, Duval and Scout encountered two black bears standing in the road. The bears refused to yield the right of way. "I screwed up my courage," Duval wrote later, "nearly breaking the screwdriver in the attempt, and resolved to pass them if I could." The bruins growled and showed their teeth but drew back to either side of the road as Duval passed between them with his knife drawn. Scout kept close by with his tail tucked between his legs.

The next morning, John C. Duval hiked four miles through the canebrake and eventually rejoined the Texas army.

The land under the canebrake proved more valuable than the cane or the wild game in it. Centuries of rotting cane stalks had given it wonderful fertility. Settlers began clearing the cane after John C. Duval helped Texas win her independence. Some invented cane-cutting devices but most resorted to burning, which provided fantastic entertainment. The air in the chambers of the cane would expand with the heat of the fire and cause multiple explosions equal in loudness to gunshots. The flames would light the night sky for miles around.

In fewer than 100 years, the great canebrake was almost completely wiped out. In 1925 only a small section of cane still existed near Wharton along the Colorado River. The panthers and lobo wolves had long since disappeared and a black bear hadn't been spotted in many years.

Four Wharton men let a dozen dogs loose in the canebrake to hunt up some bobcats. They jumped a huge black bear instead. After a chase of an hour and a half, the dogs bayed the old bear. He killed one dog and broke another's leg before the hunters could shoot him dead. He weighed 350 pounds. It was the last bear killed in the region in the last stretch of the once-great cane forest.

PART 3

WILD WEST

EARLY TEXAS RAILROADS

Everything seemed on schedule for one of Texas' first railroads in 1858. Construction crews had completed the twenty-three miles of track between Caddo Lake and Marshall by late January. The railroad company seemed sure to fulfill the obligation of its charter to have trains running by February first.

But the railroad company's new locomotive did not arrive at Caddo Lake on the riverboat as scheduled. In desperation, the company officials pored over their contract looking for a loophole, lest they should lose the charter granted by the Texas Legislature. Finally someone realized that the charter did not stipulate what mode of power the railroad had to utilize.

The company acquired three yokes of oxen and hitched them to two boxcars. The oxen hauled the boxcars to the summit of the first hill and then stopped. The engineers then loaded the oxen aboard the boxcars and let them coast down the opposite slope of the hill. The oxen were then unloaded and hitched to take the next hill, and so on for the entire twenty-three miles.

This hay-burning railroad eventually burgeoned into the Texas and Pacific Railroad Company.

Railroads meant almost certain prosperity for the towns they served. Much politicking went into a railroad's choice of routes and placement of depots. Some towns payed bonuses to the railroads to have them bypass neighboring towns.

In other cases, the trains simply wouldn't stop in one town because a rival town had paid for the privilege of having the only depot in the county, or because the railroad didn't deem the town worthy of a depot. The towns that suffered only the noise of the railroads and enjoyed none of its services usually found ways to fight back.

At Childress, the Fort Worth and Denver refused to build a depot and built one in nearby Henry instead. The Childress residents simply covered the tracks with oil which caused the locomotive's wheels to whirl uselessly. The trains stopped in Childress whether the railroad had scheduled a stop or not. As a compromise, the Fort Worth and Denver offered to move the entire town of Childress down the tracks to Henry. The residents agreed, but insisted on changing the name of Henry to Childress.

At Goree, the residents soaped the tracks when anyone in the town needed passengers or freight moved. The trains had to stop until the slippery suds dried or were rinsed away. Goree won its own depot and achieved rail service from the Wichita Valley Railroad by adopting the clean tracks policy.

The Fort Worth and Denver passed through Hall County just as Memphis and Salisbury were fighting it out for the county seat. The railroad passed through both towns but the trains only stopped at Salisbury. The Memphis folks, however, were blessed with a hill just outside of town that the trains could not negotiate when the tracks became mysteriously slippery. Soon, Memphis had its own depot and the county seat.

So it was, in the peculiar days of the railroad frontier, that trains sometimes required oxen to get them going, and soap to make them stop.

THE GREAT COMPROMISE

Today the town of Fredericksburg lies smack dab in the middle of the thickest population of whitetail deer in the world. Deer hunting represents a major part of the local economy.

Though Fredericksburg has a lot more to offer than deer hunting, it relies heavily on the sport. It is ironic, then, that the old German town owes its original existence not to hunting, but to a ban on hunting. In 1847 a hunting agreement between German emigrants and Comanche Indians was the great compromise that allowed the town to exist in peace, to grow, and to prosper.

In 1844 the German Emigration Company purchased settlement rights on almost four million acres between the Llano and the Colorado. But this land was far from the coast, so the Germans first had to establish way stations where emigrants could stop and rest during the journey to their new homes.

The first way station was New Braunfels, established in 1845. That year Baron Otfried Hans Friedherr von Meusebach became the commissioner general of the German Emigration Company. Red-haired and red-bearded, he was thirty-three years old and well-educated. When he left for Texas, he renounced his hereditary title of baron and Americanized his name to John O. Meusebach.

Meusebach's job was to get his German emigrants to the land grant between the Colorado and Llano rivers. But that land was located on the other side of about 100 miles of unsettled wilderness. Meusebach needed another way station between New Braunfels and the land grant and that way station would become known as Fredericksburg.

Meusebach explored the area himself and personally chose the site for Fredericksburg. He called it "the most beautiful part of the entire country" and bought 10,000 acres for the emigration company on credit. In 1846, 120 settlers arrived and started building.

There was just one problem. This was Comanche land. Anglo Texans of the day portrayed the Comanche as mounted, painted, howling harbingers of death; treacherous "savages" reaping a grim harvest of skull-wrenched scalps; lurking warriors who carried children away, despoiled the virtue of women, and tortured captive enemies to death.

The Germans, mostly of peasant stock, were in no way equipped to do battle with Indians. They were farmers. They had a few guns but didn't know how to use them like the Americans from Tennessee and Kentucky who had pushed into the Texas wilderness before them. The Germans knew Fredericksburg could be crushed at any time by Comanches.

Everyone in Texas, including the governor, told Meusebach to abandon his town on the dangerous Indian frontier. But Meusebach insisted on actually searching out the Comanches in order to make a treaty with them ensuring safe travel for the thousands of Germans who would soon be coming to settle the land grant between the Colorado and the Llano. In January 1847, he left Fredericksburg with forty men in search of the most feared Indians in Texas.

Meusebach crossed the Llano and, where the town of Mason now stands, encountered a band of Penateka Comanches led by Chief Ketomoczy. The chief immediately wanted to know if the whites had come to make peace or wage war, stating that either one would suit him just fine. Meusebach told Ketomoczy that he wanted to forge a great treaty with the entire Comanche nation and asked for a general council. The chief told the Germans to meet on the San Saba at the next full moon.

By March first, hundreds of Comanches had assembled on the San Saba. Meusebach had sent all but seven men back to Fredericksburg. If a conflict broke out he would be hopelessly outnumbered. When he entered the Comanche camp, Meusebach and his men ceremoniously fired their guns into the air and entered the camp with empty weapons as a sign of their trust. The head war chiefs Buffalo Hump, Old Owl, and Santana were impressed with Meusebach's bravery and honored him with an Indian name they bestowed upon him in Spanish—"El Sol Colorado"—The Red Sun.

Two days of negotiations began. Meusebach offered a three-point treaty:

Number one, the Comanches were to allow the Germans to travel safely across Indian lands. Likewise, the Indians were to be always welcomed and protected in the German towns.

Number two, both Comanches and Germans were to help each other fight outlaws or other hostile tribes.

Number three, the Germans would pay the Indians $3,000 in supplies and cash to purchase settlement rights on the Indians' hunting grounds.

A fourth point, considered minor at the time, may actually have been the key to the success of the treaty. This point dealt with hunting.

Comanches lived to hunt as surely as they hunted to live. The Germans, on the other hand, cared very little about hunting. Though deer, turkey, black bear, and buffalo could be found in the Fredericksburg area, the settlers lived on "cornmeal, beef, and coffee" as one early visitor to the town recorded. Any game they did acquire they bought from friendly Indians who hunted for them. This lack of interest in hunting by the settlers was perhaps the deciding factor that would enable two very different cultures to co-exist.

The second day of the council, the Indian chiefs accepted Meusebach's offer. A few weeks later, on May 9, 1847, the treaty was signed in Fredericksburg by six Penateka war chiefs.

Minor infringements on the treaty were committed at times by Germans and Comanches, but the treaty stood— the only treaty between Comanches and whites to succeed. The Indians hunted and sold meat and horses to the Germans, often trading for crops and store-bought supplies. Though Comanches battled other whites across west Texas, they never harmed the German towns or farms.

John O. Meusebach's treaty reveals much about the importance of hunting rights in frontier history. (The Red River War of 1874 stemmed largely from buffalo hunters invading hunting grounds Indians had secured by treaty.) It also tells us something about the Comanches. Treated fairly, they could live peaceably among settled people.

DRIFT FENCES

No fence of consequence stood between Texas and the Arctic Circle up through the middle of the 1870s. Cattle roamed at will, held in only by line riders—cowboys who rode imaginary lines across the public range to keep cattle close to their ranch headquarters.

During winter, the line riders concentrated on the southern lines of their ranges. Cattle turned south with each norther, seeking warmer weather, grass, and water, turning their tails to blizzards. The best line riders in the West couldn't hold them on their home ranges. Cowboys simply followed their herds until the storms had passed and then tried to push the cows back up north.

Cattle from Colorado, Kansas, and Indian Territory drifted onto ranges already overstocked by Texas cattlemen. They overgrazed the ranges until scarcely a blade of grass remained. Gaunt, hungry longhorns died by the thousands. In the spring, Texas cattlemen had the task of separating their surviving cattle from the northern herds.

Texas ranchers decided to end the drift. Their idea seemed reasonable. They would erect "drift fences" to the north of their ranges that would keep cattle from the north from drifting in. Then they would put drift fences to the south of their ranges to keep their own stock from drifting too far from home. The drift fences would save home range and discourage trail drivers from bringing even more cattle through in the summer.

The first extensive fencing practiced in the Panhandle consisted of drift fences. In the early 1880s ranchers began stretching barbed wire east to west in lengths of thirty miles or more. Some drift fences extended from Indian Territory to New Mexico. Soon, drift fences went up in the Pecos region. Disaster resulted.

Cold, starving cattle drifted south until they hit the fences. They bunched together, the stronger ones trampling the weaker ones to death. Carcasses of dead bovines piled up higher than the fences. Some cattle managed to climb over the frozen, snow-covered piles of carrion against the fences and escape to the south until they hit the next drift fence.

In the winter of 1883-84, carcasses blocked the Arkansas River. U.S. soldiers dragged 6,000 head from the Concho River. The die-off amounted to 25 percent. The next winter almost half the cattle on the ranges died of starvation. A year later, one rancher turned out 11,000 head to find only 800 alive in spring. By 1886-87, mortality was still at 40 percent.

To make matters worse, fence wars broke out over the legality of private fences on public range. Fence cutters destroyed wire barriers almost as fast as the fencers could put them up. Texas began to see the evils of drift fencing.

But the fences had invaded, and the open-range days were over. A new type of stock-raising was in order. Ranges fell into private ownership. The windmill allowed the fencing in of any pasture with underground water available. Advancing railroads began to make the long cattle drives unnecessary. Cattle were given winter food and shelter, and controlled breeding programs were introduced.

However disastrous they might have proven, drift fences had provided the bridge needed to move the beef industry from the open-range days to the big pasture era.

FENCE WARS

The practice of fencing previously open range threw Texas into turmoil in the 1880s. Cowboys turned on employers who threatened to replace them with fences. Neighboring cattlemen on friendly terms suddenly split over fencing disagreements. Some large ranchers and "little men," formerly at odds with one another, suddenly began cooperating in cutting stretches of fence.

Most wealthy ranchers who were opposed to fencing had made their fortunes on free grassland. The little men could not survive without it. Bing Grimes, for example, owned only eleven acres but had one of the largest herds on the Texas coast. He relied on free range to feed his cattle.

The fence wars made for some strange bedfellows. Some ranchers welcomed rustlers into fence cutting organizations. The rustlers joined antifence factions because they found stealing beeves much simpler without fences getting in the way.

Antifence groups made up of big men, little men, and rustlers banded together to fight a common enemy—the fencer. A few upstart cattlemen had bought large tracts of formerly free range from the state and fenced it in—keeping the herds of others out. They fenced in water holes, too. They arrogantly fenced across cattle trails to the rail heads, even across public roads.

The free-range advocates fought back with pliers, or "nippers," as they called them. They formed secret fence cutting mobs with names like "Hatchet Company" and "Rolling Fence Cutters" and "Blue Devils."

Fence cutters used many creative methods. Some clipped every strand between all the posts, making the former fence look like "a vicious animal maddened so that every particular hair stood up on end." Some pulled the posts up as well.

Other antifence groups left painted signs on fences. One in Falls County read, "We, the wire cutters, inform you not to fence no pasture land, for we will not suffer for it any longer." Some fence cutters went so far as to "lift" or remove the wire completely. Frank Luther, once the mayor of Cimarron, told what happened when he "borrowed" a strand on one occasion. He was working his way up one side of a hill, pulling staples from a few posts at a time, then rolling the wire to that point. Near the top of the hill, Luther noticed a tug on the same strand he was lifting. He peeked over the crest and couldn't believe his eyes.

"Coming up the opposite slope of the hill," Luther said, "swiping the same top wire I was working on, was the Methodist preacher of Cimarron's only church!"

Bills were introduced by profencers to allow shooting any fence cutter on the spot or arresting anyone carrying pliers. The legislature dealt with the issue more moderately in a special session. It decided to keep all public roads free of fences, require a gate on every third mile of fence on public range, and make fence-cutting a felony. The Texas Rangers enforced the new laws effectively.

Gradually the state-owned public lands were bought by private citizens, and the open range days in Texas faded. Many ranchers who had grazed their herds on government lands instead of buying their own spreads had to leave Texas. Bing Grimes was one example. An old enemy of his, Shanghai Pierce, had bought and fenced all the free range Grimes had once used. Grimes was forced to sell his eleven acres and start over in Indian Territory.

FENCE PHONES

Barbwire did more than enclose pastures and turn beeves toward the end of the nineteenth century. It carried some of the first telephone conversations to cross remote regions of the West.

The McKay brothers, Guy and Wallace, had a ranch way up in Handsford County, Texas, where the Texas and Oklahoma panhandles meet. Their ranch houses were fifteen miles apart, and communication consisted mostly of messages sent by way of fence-riding cowboys. About 1898 the McKays realized something about barbwire. Though it covered long stretches of lonely country, it eventually led to all the pockets of habitation. One particular stretch ran straight from Guy's house to Wallace's.

The McKay brothers ordered a couple of phone boxes from Boston. They didn't have to string any wire. They already had strand after strand of it running between their homes. They hooked the phone boxes to the top strand of barbwire running between their houses, plugged ground wires into the earth to complete the circuit, and invited all their neighbors over to test the contraption. They all got a new thrill out of talking to relatives and acquaintances fifteen miles away, though the system tended to pick up a lot of static from the ground.

The primitive barbwire telephone could save ranchers and cowboys many unnecessary trips, and it didn't even come with a phone bill. Many ranchers began buying phone boxes, and even people in the towns hooked up to the barbwire system.

No central station existed, so when a caller cranked the magneto on a phone box, sending an electric jolt through the wire, all the phones on the circuit rang, and everyone on the system might answer at the same time to find out who the call was for. To minimize the confusion, the barbwire phone users developed their own specific sequences of long and short rings. To signal a particular household, callers had to crank a special ring sequence—two short rings, a long ring, and another short ring, for example.

Cowboys who rode fence lines paid special attention to the top strand of wire to keep the phones in good working order. When the fence came to a gate or a barbwire gap, ranchers installed a high fence post on either side of the passage. They then ran the top strand of barbwire over the high posts so livestock and riders could pass underneath without breaking the phone circuit.

When a splice had to be made in the top strand of barbwire, fence builders wound an extra piece of wire around one side of the splice, crossed over the joint, and then wound it around on the other side to make certain that a good connection existed through the splice.

Normally, the barbwire telephone failed to function only when it rained. Wet fence posts grounded the system out. There was one other drawback. The fence-mending cowboy who happened to latch on to the top strand of barbwire just as some ranch house resident cranked a magneto, found out what it meant to get his bell rung.

BATTLE OF THE NECHES

The Cherokees had lived in East Texas for twenty years under the wise leadership of the great Chief Bowles. They held a hunk of fertile land between the Neches and Angelina rivers. They had come from the Carolinas on the Trail of Tears, through Arkansas, to settle finally in the pine forests of East Texas. Sam Houston, president of the Republic, held a fast friendship with Chief Bowles.

Houston's successor, Mirabeau Lamar, cared less for the Cherokees. In 1839 he found a good excuse to run them out of Texas. Texas Rangers had killed a Mexican agent near Austin. On his body the rangers found a document suggesting the Cherokees would join a plot to overthrow the Republic through Mexican and Indian cooperation.

A commission of high-ranking Texans went to East Texas to negotiate the removal of the Cherokees. They told Bowles to leave peacefully or his tribe would be forced out. Bowles denied the charges against his tribe, including local accusations that Cherokee braves had massacred two white families. The eighty-three-year-old chief warned that his men would surely vote to wage war rather than retreat.

The Cherokees recruited warriors from the Delawares, Shawnees, Kickapoos, and other tribes. The elite of the Texas military—including Vice President David G. Burnet; Secretary of War Albert Sidney Johnston; and Generals Hugh McCloud, Thomas Jefferson Rusk, Kelsey Douglas, and Edward Burleson—closed in on the Cherokees.

On the evening of July 15, the Texans found the Cherokees in a creek bed a few miles west of Tyler. A short battle claimed the lives of two Texans and eighteen Cherokees. The Indians moved northward overnight.

The next morning the Texas forces sent numerous detachments to protect the families of settlers. They expected the Indians to break up and engage in scattered, strike-and-retreat attacks like Comanches were famous for. The main force of the Texas army fell in number to about 500.

The Indians, however, stayed in one group, numbering about 800. The Texans found them ready to fight in a ravine near the Neches River. Throughout the ensuing two-hour Battle of the Neches, Chief Bowles rode behind his front line of warriors adorned conspicuously with a sword and sash, a silk vest, and a military hat—all given to him by Sam Houston.

When the warriors retreated at last, Bowles' horse collapsed from wounds. The chief also had a wound in his thigh. As he tried to get away, a Texan shot him in the back. The old chief fell, then sat up to face the charging Texans. A captain shot Bowles in the head.

The Indians suffered about 100 killed and many more wounded. Six Texans died and thirty-six sustained wounds. Vice President Burnet received minor wounds.

The Indians scattered to Mexico, Arkansas, and Indian Territory. The settled areas of Texas were now free of Indians except for the Alabamas and the Coushattas, who were forced onto less fertile lands but allowed to stay.

CODE DUELLO

When disagreements occurred between gentlemen of early Texas, the "Code Duello" often came into play. The code was an unwritten set of rules for conducting duels on the "field of honor." During the days of the Texas Republic, duels were so common that Texans considered such an event a mere "difficulty" or an "affray."

The city of Houston produced such a proliferation of "difficulties" that a designated dueling ground became recognized within the city limits. J.H. Herdon noticed an unusual incident in Houston one day in 1838 and recorded it in his diary: "No affray on this day."

An insult, often over some seemingly inconsequential matter, usually brought the Code Duello into use. The insulted party issued a challenge to his detractor. The challenged man had the right to choose the location, time, weapons, and all other terms of the duel. Each duelist chose at least one "second" to witness the fight and see that it was conducted properly. Sometimes the seconds were peacemakers. Sometimes they wound up fighting, too. Surgeons often attended the duels for obvious reasons.

Jim Bowie once served as a second in a duel fought on the banks of the Mississippi River. Each side in the affray included four seconds and a surgeon. The fight became a free-for-all, and Bowie was shot four times and cut in five places. When a man rushed him with a sword, Bowie rose and stabbed the man with his Bowie knife. Two men were killed and two badly wounded in this duel. Bowie spent months recovering from wounds.

According to the Code Duello, nothing could stop a duel once it was arranged, unless the challenger withdrew his challenge or the other party apologized for whatever it was the duel was being fought over.

A remarkable sense of fair play existed in most duels. In one, the distance was set at five paces because one of the combatants was extremely near-sighted.

A prominent early Texas citizen, Dr. Branch T. Archer, fought a duel in Virginia in which he wounded his opponent in the right arm with the first round of firing. The wounded man was still not satisfied and, calling for another round of shooting, shifted the pistol to his left hand. To ensure a fair fight, Dr. Archer also shot left-handed in the second round and killed his opponent.

During the Texas Revolution one officer in the Texas army killed another in a duel over which cuts of beef their respective companies would receive.

Two of the highest ranking officers in the Texas army were Generals Albert Sidney Johnston and Felix Huston, and they were good friends. But when Sam Houston became president of Texas and chose Johnston to lead the Texas army, Felix Huston felt injury to his honor and challenged his friend Johnston to a duel. If Johnston had refused, he would have lost the respect of his army. In the duel, Johnston fell with a hip wound and barely survived.

Sam Houston himself was plagued by challenges. He had fought and won a duel in Nashville in 1827, but the experience had soured him on the barbaric ritual. While others practiced their dueling skills, Houston cultivated the art of avoiding duels with honor. Old Sam once received a written challenge and handed it to his secretary saying, "This is number twenty-four. The angry gentleman must wait his turn."

The Code Duello said that a gentleman could refuse a challenge issued by an individual of inferior courage. As the Hero of San Jacinto, the bravest man in Texas, Houston could use this rule on just about anybody. To avoid a duel with David G. Burnet, Sam said, "Tell him I won't fight him, for I never fight downhill."

When challenged to a knife fight, face-to-face, by William H. Wharton, Sam Houston shouted, "Draw if you dare! Lift your hand against the majesty of Texas and the Almighty God would blast you where you stand!" Wharton backed down.

If Sam Houston spent considerable energy avoiding duels, an earlier Texan, Strap Buckner, spent as much energy trying to get into them. Strap once wanted to fight with rifles at ten paces because a camp mate prematurely removed a piece of meat from a pot of boiling water. Strap liked it well done.

On another occassion, while herding a *caballada* of horses up from the Rio Grande, Buckner challenged his partner, Joshua Parker, to a duel over some trifling matter. Because darkness had fallen, Parker suggested they postpone the duel until dawn. Strap reluctantly agreed and the two men went to sleep.

Strap woke his opponent at sunrise, eager to shoot it out. Parker stretched and said, "Buckner, I have been thinking upon this matter and have come to the conclusion that we had better not fight, for if we should both fall, what in hell would become of the *caballada*?"

Strap had a quick temper but he also had a sense of humor. He had cooled down overnight and withdrew his challenge.

Noah Smithwick played an unusual role in a duel that occurred in San Felipe during Texas' colonial days. Two men, Moore and McKinstry, had agreed to settle their differences on the field of honor with pistols. Since Smithwick was a gunsmith and a good pistol shot, both came to him for training.

The method of practice for the duel involved tacking a ribbon the height of a man against the trunk of a tree. Both men came around to take their shots at the ribbon under Smithwick's instruction. Moore cut the tape with regularity while McKinstry seldom even hit the tree. "I looked upon McKinstry as a virtual dead man," wrote Smithwick.

But when the most vital shots flew during the course of the actual duel, Moore missed his target completely and then had both legs broken by the pistol ball of McKinstry. A friend of Smithwick's explained the unpredicted outcome: "The tree had no pistol pointed at Moore when he was shooting at it."

The Code Duello held on in Texas until Civil War days and even a little beyond. By this time, though, the revolver had been improved and metallic cartridges were in use. The old single-shot dueling pistol—a weapon created solely for dueling—became obsolete. The six-shooter—a gun of many uses—was carried in a holster almost everywhere the man of the frontier ventured, unlike the dueling pistol, which was usually kept in a box until needed. This ready access to six shots was one of the factors that caused dueling to deteriorate into gun-fighting.

One of the last great Texas duelists who made the transition to gunfighter was Clay Allison. One of his gunfights in New Mexico reveals how rapid-fire weapons did away with the duel and led to gunslinging instead.

A fellow named Bill Chunk beat Allison in a horse race and made him mad. They agreed to fight a duel by mounting their horses, riding toward each other at full speed, and shooting on the gallop.

Just then the dinner bell rang at the hotel where both men were staying, and they decided to eat first "to see that the dead one goes to hell with a full stomach," as Chunk reportedly put it. During the meal, Chunk reached under the table for his napkin and instead brought up his pistol which he fired at Allison. He missed. Allison drew his revolver, killed Chunk, and went on with his meal.

Dueling and dueling pistols went out of fashion and the gentlemanly, barbaric Code Duello was dead by Clay Allison's time. Social changes and improvements in weapons put an end to the demand for dueling pistols until finally they were owned only by collectors.

ADOBE WALLS

The great herds of buffalo in Kansas had vanished by 1874, so the hide hunters came to the Texas Panhandle. They constructed a crude hide town near the adobe ruins of an abandoned trading post called Adobe Walls.

Meanwhile, Isa-Tai, an ambitious young Comanche medicine man, had created a "bulletproof" yellow war paint. Seven hundred warriors from five tribes prepared to use his magic and wage war on the Adobe Walls hunters who were slaughtering their buffalo.

In the early morning hours of June 27, one woman and twenty-eight men slept at Adobe Walls. At two o'clock a loud crack rang out from Jim Hanrahan's saloon and the proprietor yelled, "Clear out! The ridgepole is breaking!" About fifteen men rallied to bolster the main support for the sod roof. Afterward, Hanrahan called for drinks on the house.

The men were still drinking at dawn when some 700 Indians attacked the settlement. The following five-day siege claimed the lives of four buffalo hunters and about thirty Indians, and was characterized by feats of strength, courage, and marksmanship on both sides.

As one wounded Comanche warrior fell, Chief Quanah Parker galloped before the muzzles of the big buffalo guns to rescue his tribesman. Clinging to his mount with one hand and one foot, Quanah extended his free hand downward, hoisted the fallen warrior, and carried him to safety.

In the store of Charlie Rath, one mortally wounded man called feebly for water. Finally, elderly Billy Keeler said, "Give me a bucket," and climbed through a window.

Keeler reached the hand pump in the stockade and filled the bucket in the midst of an Indian fusillade. Old Man Keeler's dog fell between his feet with twenty bullet holes in its body, but Keeler seemed to manifest Isa-Tai's bulletproof magic with more success than any of the Indians. He made it back to the store with the water. The wounded man took a drink and died. The other buffalo hunters had to hold Keeler down to keep him from crawling back out through the window to avenge the death of his dog.

On the third day of the siege, Billy Dixon, a marksman among marksmen, saw several mounted Indians on a distant bluff. He squeezed off his famous "mile-long shot" that knocked an Indian from his horse at 1,538 yards. Dixon's shot effectively ended the fighting.

Years later Billy Dixon met Quanah Parker and they discussed the battle.

Isa-Tai, the disgraced shaman, claimed that a Cheyenne warrior had violated a taboo by killing a skunk before the battle, rendering his bulletproof war paint and the rest of his magic useless. After the battle, he was dubbed "That Comical Fellow" and was generally ridiculed by the Indians.

After many years, Jim Hanrahan claimed that his pistol, not his ridgepole, had shattered the early morning silence before the attack. He had tricked the men into rising early that morning because an army scout had warned him of the impending Indian attack. He had not passed the warning on to the hunters for fear they would bolt for Dodge City and his Adobe Walls business would fail.

Despite his fierce instincts for entrepreneurial survival, Hanrahan's business—and the entire hide town of Adobe Walls—died anyway.

THE BUFFALO WALLOW FIGHT

Comanche and Kiowa Indians swarmed everywhere across the Panhandle during the "Red River War" of 1874. A party of two scouts and four soldiers carrying dispatches from field headquarters to Fort Supply had to travel at night and hide during the day to keep their scalps. But, at dawn on September 12, they surmounted a knoll and blundered into a large war party.

Bullets flew immediately. The Indians surrounded the army men on the bare hillside. And Indian marksman shot Trooper George Smith, who was holding the horses. They stampeded with much of the soldiers' gear. A bullet shattered the knee of scout Amos Chapman. The other scout, Billy Dixon, felt lucky to have only one wound through his calf. His shirt was riddled with near misses.

The men returned the Indian fire all morning. As the hostiles closed in, Billy Dixon—who had recently earned renown for his "mile-long shot" at the Battle of Adobe Walls—spotted a dried up buffalo wallow and sprinted for it through the whirr of slugs. The other men followed, except for Smith and Chapman, who were too badly wounded. The men in the buffalo wallow dug in with knives and bare hands.

Smith was thought to be dead, but when Dixon learned from a soldier in the wallow that Chapman's knee was shattered, he decided to rescue his fellow scout. Several times he tried, but Indian gunfire drove him back to the buffalo wallow each time. Finally, Dixon abandoned all caution and reached Chapman through the spray of lead. He loaded

Chapman, who was larger than he was, onto his back and carried the wounded man to the wallow.

Amos Chapman and the other wounded men disregarded their injuries and continued to fight. By 3:00 in the afternoon, ammunition had run low and the wounded were suffering from lack of water. Salvation came from the west in the form of a dark rain cloud. Rain water swirled into the depression pawed out by bison, and the men drank from it though their own blood colored the muddy pools.

The Indians called off the attack and sat huddled under blankets. The soldiers had no coats or even hats to turn the chilly rain and wind.

Before nightfall Trooper Rath volunteered to fetch Smith's pistol and ammunition belt. He returned with the astonishing news that Smith was still alive. Rath and Dixon carried Smith to the wallow where he died during the night. The men rested on piled sagebrush to cushion against the damp ground.

At dawn, Billy Dixon slipped away from the buffalo wallow and found a troop supply train which sent rescue almost two days later. George Smith was buried beside the wallow. Amos Chapman lost his left leg but continued to ride as well as ever with his wooden leg. All the men in the Buffalo Wallow Fight received the Medal of Honor.

Billy Dixon, in his autobiography, reflected on his most perilous adventure: "Every night the same stars are shining way out there in the Panhandle, the winds sigh as mournfully as they did then, and I often wonder if a single settler who passes the lonely spot knows how desperately six men once battled for their lives . . ."

WIND WAGONS

An old Sioux tribesman in the Dakotas, after the fall of
the Sioux nation, told writer Stanley Vestal a peculiar legend. The Arapahos, said the old Indian, once befriended a
white man who rode a huge, wheeled vehicle that moved
faster than a stampeding buffalo without benefit of draft
animals. It didn't belch smoke or follow steel tracks the way
the Iron Horse did, and the driver rode on top behind a flag
the size of a thirteen-skin tepee.

Vestal dismissed the yarn as second-hand mythology.

But the records of white men, as Vestal would one day
discover, also described wagons that moved independent of
harnessed livestock—Gail Borden's "Terraqueous Machine," for example.

Retiring from public office in Galveston, 1843, Gail
Borden became a full-time inventor. His first stroke of genius was an amphibious wagon rigged with a mast, a square
sail, a rudder, and some kind of steering device for the front
wheels.

The first public run of the terraqueous machine occurred before a crowd on a stretch of Galveston beach. A
crew of the inventor's closest friends rode with him. When
Borden made sail, a gust billowed the canvas, and faint-
hearted passengers became frantic over the velocity. Then
Borden abruptly decided to test the seaworthiness of his
vessel. He angled sharply into the surf. The passengers panicked—it seems Borden had forgotten to mention the
amphibious adaptations of his vehicle. The frightened crew
scrambled to one side and upset the balance of the vessel. It
dumped them all, uninjured, into shallow water.

The debacle forced Borden out of transportation and into foods. In 1856 he won a patent for his process of condensing milk in a vacuum and plotted the course for the Borden Milk Company.

But canvas-rigged prairie schooners didn't disappear from the West with the failure of the terraqueous machine. A former sailor from California retired from his maritime adventures and moved to the Southern Plains in 1888. The gusty prairies made "Old Man Wallace" long for a billowing sheet of canvas, so he acquired one. He also bought a light spring wagon, affixed a mast, rigged a steering system, and began pleasure cruising on the High Plains.

The land sailor furled his sail beside the homestead of G.L. Browning one day and asked the farmer to climb in and act as a human ballast to keep his wagon from blowing over in the high winds. The telegraph poles along the road to Amarillo went by so fast they resembled teeth on a fine-toothed comb, Browning wrote later, in a letter to a friend. The sailing surrey clamored into town sounding like "the clatter of wheels of hell" and frightened twenty cow ponies away from a hitching rail.

Wallace had no plans for mass-producing his invention, but another erstwhile sailor, "Windwagon Thomas," had more ambition. He proposed an entire fleet that would force the ox and mule trains into obsolescence on the Santa Fe Trail.

Westport (Kansas City) was trailhead for the old trade route, and Thomas's home port. Making a 300-mile round trip in a light wind wagon, Thomas fetched Council Grove without a hitch in 1853 and convinced a group of investors to form the Overland Navigation Company. They financed the first in a planned fleet of "super-windwagons."

The modified tongue of a huge freight wagon became a tiller. The vessel would ride tailgate-first over the waves of prairie grasses on twelve-foot-diameter wheels. A twenty-foot mast stepped on the foredeck was rigged with a boom and triangular mainsail.

With Windwagon Thomas at the helm, his investors boarded the prairie schooner for her maiden voyage. The wheeled wonder cruised before the wind on a beam reach at speeds alarming to men accustomed to nothing faster than a good saddle horse.

When the skipper gave his vessel full starboard rudder to bring her around in order to tack her against the wind, the stiff breeze filled the wrong side of the mainsail and sent the windwagon cruising in reverse. Then the wagon tongue jammed and the flagship of the Overland Navigation Company plotted its own aimless course toward Turkey Creek. The financial directors of the corporation abandoned their partnership by leaping from the twelve-foot-high deck. Windwagon Thomas went down with the ship as she ran aground against a stake-and-rider fence.

When Stanley Vestal read the saga of Windwagon Thomas and his "Dryland Navy" in a 1905 edition of the *Kansas City Star*, he suddenly remembered the old Sioux legend of the white man among the Arapahos. The *Star* article said Windwagon Thomas sailed off into the sunset, toward Arapaho country, after his corporation sank. Vestal tried to link Thomas with the Indian legend, but his old Sioux informer had died, and the legend had blown away on the trade winds of the plains.

LIEUTENANT FLIPPER

Henry Ossian Flipper wasn't the first black man to attend West Point, but he was the first to graduate. Born to Georgia slave parents in 1856, Flipper was lucky enough to begin an informal education, tutored by a slave, at age eight. Later, while attending Atlanta University, Flipper applied for appointment to West Point and was accepted in 1873.

The press and the public treated Flipper as a curiosity, often badgering him incessantly. But Flipper withstood his difficult tenure at West Point and graduated in 1877, becoming the first black officer in the U.S. Army.

Lieutenant Flipper's orders brought him to Texas with the Tenth United States Cavalry, then to Fort Sill, Indian Territory. He supervised engineering projects, drained ponds, built roads, and installed telegraph lines. His superiors praised him for his conduct in the campaign against Apache war chief Victorio.

Flipper's education at West Point emphasized geology, mineralogy, and engineering, and he excelled in those fields. But the Army soon appointed him post quartermaster and commissary officer, responsible for housing, water, fuel, transportation, clothing, equipment, and food at Fort Davis, Texas. Flipper had little training in accounting and bookkeeping methods.

In 1881 over one thousand dollars in Fort Davis commissary funds disappeared. Post commander William R. Shafter had Flipper arrested. A court-martial tried Flipper for embezzlement and for conduct unbecoming of an officer. His prosecutors failed to prove the embezzlement charge, but the court-martial found Flipper guilty of the nebulous "conduct" offense. His sentence was discharge from the Army.

Flipper theorized that a fellow officer framed him by stealing the missing commissary funds. He also suspected the "conduct" charge stemmed from his friendship with a young white woman, the sister-in-law of a Fort Davis officer, whom he often accompanied on riding excursions.

Henry Flipper attempted for years, unsuccessfully, to appeal his conviction and regain his military commission. However, his court-martial far from ruined his life. He became a prominent land surveyor and mining engineer and worked extensively in Mexico. He also served the Justice Department as a special land claims agent, investigating cases of fraud involving old Spanish land grants. He became fluent in Spanish and translated a collection of Spanish and Mexican laws dating from the sixteenth century.

In the twentieth century, Henry Flipper worked for numerous mining and oil companies and traveled from Alaska to Venezuela to Spain. He returned to Atlanta in 1930 and died there in 1940. His epitaph could have come from his own autobiography, written at Fort Sill:

"Will prejudice ever be obliterated from the minds of the people? Will man ever cease to prejudge his fellow being for color's sake alone? Grant, O merciful God, that he may!"

On his death certificate, Henry Ossian Flipper's brother listed his occupation as "Retired Army Officer."

INDIAN SIGN LANGUAGE

William Tomkins, a sign language expert who lived among the Sioux from 1884-1894, described sign talk as "the world's most easily learned language because it is elemental, basic, logical, and the signs in general are what should properly be made to illustrate the idea." He also called it a "skeleton language of ideas."

Some of the earliest white explorers on the continent reported seeing the sign language in use. It was common to tribes as far south as Mexico and as far north as Canada, from the Atlantic to the Pacific shores. Some Indian legends said the language came from the south and the Comanches in particular claimed they had learned it in Mexico. Other tribes believed the Kiowas had invented the language. The nomadic Indians between the Rockies and the Mississippi were the best sign talkers, and the Kiowas were right in the middle of them on the plains and were considered the most accomplished signers.

Many theories have been offered to explain why sign language evolved in the first place. Some anthropologists believe it was started to aid ancient hunters in getting close to game without being heard. Others believe warfare brought about the language. Indians could use it to communicate silently near an enemy camp and plan an attack.

While the signs certainly have their advantages in hunting and warfare, trade was most probably responsible for the development of the so-called "universal sign language" of the American Indians. One sign language expert maintained that over 500 languages were spoken among some seventy distinct cultural families. Even tribes that hunted and fought together often spoke different languages.

The Southern Arapaho and Southern Cheyenne, for example, often went hunting together, fought together, and shared the same villages, yet neither could speak the other's language. They communicated with signs. The universal sign language allowed almost all Indians to communicate with members of other tribes, trade with them, and ask about friends or enemies.

"The beauty of sign talk," wrote William Tomkins, "depends upon the manner of making gestures. Movements should not be angular or jerky, but should rather be rounded and sweeping in their rendition."

For most signers, though, the language was simply a practical and necessary way to communicate. When several Indian chiefs made a trip to Washington, D.C., in the last century to meet the Great White Father, they happened to visit a school for the deaf while touring the city. They were able almost instantly to converse with the deaf students, the Indians using the Indian sign language and the students using the sign language of the deaf.

There were a few minor differences in the signs among the tribes, but the Indians never seemed to have trouble learning each other's little quirks. They also added many words during recorded history, mostly due to exposure to the white man's ways. Indians liked to keep things simple. They often used compound words to label some new object or idea and therefore didn't have to invent any new signs. They just combined old ones. Many of these compound words are familiar to us today: pale-face, iron-horse, fire-water.

Colonel Richard I. Dodge, who spent many years fighting and studying Indians, said the sign for "coffee" consisted of five signs compounded. To the Indian, coffee was the bean that you put in a pot on the fire and boiled so you could drink it. To make the sign for coffee, then, sign talkers had to sign "bean," "pot," "put on the fire," "boil," and "drink."

Dodge reported that most Indians could sign for hours with one hand while holding the reins of their horses. About 85 percent of the signs were made with the right hand alone. He also said that almost anyone could quickly pick up enough signs to communicate with the Indians. But, he added, only the old or middle-aged men were completely fluent in the language.

These experts, Dodge wrote, "will make the five signs necessary to express coffee almost as quickly as that word can be uttered."

Later, however, when the coffee mill was introduced to Indians, the sign talkers developed a new sign representing coffee, simply using a motion of one hand as if turning the crank on a coffee grinder.

THE OVERLAND STAGE

When the first Butterfield Overland Stagecoach left St. Louis bound for San Francisco on September 16, 1858, Waterman L. Ormsby rode with it. Ormsby, a twenty-three-year-old reporter for the New York *Herald*, was the first passenger to complete the historic 2,700-mile route, including 700 miles between the Red River and the Rio Grande.

Mules were used to pull the stagecoaches over the frontier portions of the route because, to Indians, mules were less attractive than horses as potential property items. One team of mules had been trained to come to feed at the sound of a large gong. The stage driver planned to use the gong to call the mules back in case Indians stole them.

Ormsby said wild, unbroken mules were used over much of the frontier. It took thirty minutes to harness each of the four wild mules in a team. "By the time a mule was caught and harnessed, often nearly choked to death, he was almost always nearly tired out before his work had commenced," wrote Ormsby.

Fresh teams were available at stage stations. One team of wild mules frightened Ormsby into walking, then tore the top off the stagecoach. The coaches regularly turned over along rough portions of the route, injuring or even killing passengers.

Passengers had only two or three chances to bathe along the entire route, and they had to catch what sleep they could in the moving stagecoach. "Sleep is shy for the first week," one stage rider reported, "but after that the passengers get used to the thing and could sleep if the coach were tumbling a precipice."

Englishman William Tallack traversed the overland route eastbound in 1860. Tallack said he and his fellow passengers slept by "sometimes slinging our feet by loops from the top of the wagon, or letting them hang over the sides between the wheels . . . and not seldom nodding for hours together in attitudes grotesque and diverse."

Conductors who managed the U.S. Mail rode in 500-mile intervals. Drivers rode in shorter stretches. Coaches were changed about every 300 miles. Top speed was about twelve miles per hour, but often the coach made no better than two or three miles per hour. Passengers had to walk once or twice a day but enjoyed the exercise. The entire trip usually took twenty-two days. A single wagon and team would require three or four months to cover the same distance.

Stage station meals beyond the frontier usually consisted of jerked beef, short bread, black coffee, and sometimes eggs or dried apples. In more civilized areas, the fare included "bread, tea, and fried steaks of bacon, venison, antelope, or mule flesh—the latter tough enough." On the eastern end of the line, delicacies such as corn, potatoes, pies, and honeycomb could be had.

Passengers paid about $150 for the entire trip, plus meals. Waterman L. Ormsby, the first passenger to ride the entire route, proclaimed it a successful venture and said he would be willing to repeat the journey, however fatiguing, at any time. He then returned to New York via Panama.

CHRISTMAS 1888

Will and Florence Harrington built their ranch house ninety miles south of a tent city called Amarillo. Will got the board and batten walls up before the first blizzard of 1888 struck. The Harringtons' nearest neighbors were line riders from a place called Sod Camp on the sprawling XIT Ranch. Women and children were few in the open range country. Florence and the two little Harrington girls were doted on by the XIT cowboys living far from mothers and sisters.

Freighters from Amarillo brought mail at unreliable intervals. As Christmas neared, Florence began watching the low spot between the hills where the wagons always appeared first. She had ordered gifts for the girls to be delivered by freight wagon. Will told her not to worry, there was still time.

But Christmas eve arrived and the freight wagons failed to appear between the hills. The girls were misty-eyed in anticipation of the holiday treats they expected to get. Florence stayed at her window all day, watching for freighters.

Will drove his wagon to the canyon and cut enough firewood to brighten the house all of Christmas day. He took his rifle, too, and managed to get within range of an antelope without much trouble. But antelope steak was everyday fare and the hearth stayed warm almost daily in December anyway. It wouldn't make up for the lack of gifts.

Snow began to fall. Will returned at sundown to find Florence standing in the front yard, watching for wagons, snow collecting on her shawl.

After the girls went to bed, Will collected a few valuable scraps of lumber and fashioned them into a little makeshift table. Florence salvaged broken china for a second-hand tea set. Some old toys were cleaned, mended, repaired, polished.

The parents arranged the meager Christmas truck and looked at it dolefully. They couldn't bear to think of their girls waking to such scant Christmas offerings. Will left the house solemnly to chop wood. Florence sat before the fire and fretted. Suddenly, snow swirled across the threshold. Will stood in the open doorway with his axe still in hand. "Do you hear something?" he asked. Florence turned a hopeful ear to the prairie. Voices. Singing! Christmas was coming!

The XIT cowboys rode into the yard with a rousing Christmas carol. They had come all the way from Yellow House, Spring Lake, and Sod Camp to spread the spirit of the season. They knew the freight had yet to arrive, and the girls would not have Christmas unless they brought it themselves.

They stuffed stockings with striped candy, oranges, apples, walnuts, and pecans. A Scotsman staying at Yellow House had brought illustrated newspapers all the way from London. The boys tuned up fiddles and guitars and the Harrington household rang with holiday cheer.

The freight wagons didn't make it to the Harrington Ranch by Christmas of 1888. But Christmas got there anyway.

PART 4

WILD CRITTERS

THE NIMROD'S WEST

"I was young—not twenty-eight years of age; and my boyish brain-cells were stored to bursting with tales of Red Indians and grizzly b'ars; caballeros and haciendas, prairies and buffaloes, Texans and Mexicans . . . I was in search of such sport and adventure as, under the circumstances, were to be found."

So wrote Windham Thomas Wyndham-Quin—Fourth Earl of Dunraven, Second Baron Kenry of the United Kingdom, Knight of the Order of St. Patrick, and Companion of the Order of St. Michael—about his feelings en route to America in 1869.

"Lord Dunraven," as he was known, was on his way to the Wild West to go hunting. His guide, year after year, on hunt after hunt, was Texas Jack Omohundro, the famous part-Indian guide, scout, and showman who in his day was just as famous as Buffalo Bill Cody and Wild Bill Hickock.

With Texas Jack, and various other characters, Lord Dunraven hunted wild plains and mountains from Colorado to Nova Scotia. He killed bear, elk, moose, deer, antelope, caribou, and any other species of game he could find in his rifle sights.

On an 1874 hunting and fishing excursion into newly established Yellowstone Park, Lord Dunraven took along two guides, two servants, a personal physician, an artist, and his brother. Such an expedition was typical of rich foreigners who came to the West for hunting thrills.

Perhaps the first of the great nimrods to invade the West was Sir William Drummond Stewart, a Scotsman who hunted from New Mexico to Oregon 1833-1843. As was the custom of rich sportsmen from abroad, Stewart hired the ablest guides he could find, such as Jim Bridger and Bill Sublette—both legendary mountain men. Stewart especially liked hunting in the Green River country of what is now Wyoming, and he attended several mountain men reunions. Between hunting trips, he resided in St. Louis or New Orleans where he entered into various business ventures.

In 1838 Stewart became "Sir William Drummond," inheriting a large estate in Scotland. He returned there, taking two live buffalos, a live grizzly bear, and two Indian braves with him.

But by 1843 Sir William was back in the Rockies for a final expedition, his most lavish ever. He hired Bill Sublette as guide and allowed three foreign naturalists to tag along. He hired a New Orleans newspaper columnist to keep a journal of the expedition. Numerous friends and family members also came along for the adventure. In all, the party included about sixty men, forty carts, two wagons, and a huge red tent furnished like an apartment where Sir William took his tea every afternoon.

After Stewart set the example for extravagances, the parties of nimrods got bigger, and the slaughter of game only increased. In 1854 Sir George Gore came west with 40 employees, 112 horses, 3 milk cows, and who knows how many cases of champagne. He hired Jim Bridger as his guide, and they spent three years bathing Wyoming Territory with the blood of the game they killed, including 40 grizzlies and 2,500 buffalo. They lost count of the deer, antelope, and elk bagged. Finally, the U.S government asked Gore to go away. His wanton slaughter of game was about to cause the Indians in Wyoming to go on the warpath.

Foreigners were not the only dudes who came west to spray bullets at game. Rich Easterners also took part in the slaughter. Among them was Teddy Roosevelt, who as a young Harvard graduate in 1883, decided he would go west and shoot a buffalo before they were extinct. By the time he became president, Teddy had killed at least one of everything considered fair game in the West. His brother got in on the act, too, hunting buffalo in the Texas Panhandle and coursing wild turkeys across the High Plains with greyhounds.

Texas was often a first or last stop on big expeditions, as the nimrods could sail to or from ports of entry such as Houston, Galveston, and Indianola (destroyed by a hurricane in 1886).

In the early 1880s, for example, a particular group of English noblemen staged a whirlwind fling across the West and ended up at Indianola. They aimed to spend ten final days of hunting on the coast.

The aristocratic sportsmen chartered a yacht to take them down the coast where "the music of our guns soon woke the echoes of this unfrequented shore." One good wingshooter in the bunch arose early one morning and brought in twenty ducks before breakfast.

They rowed a skiff along the shore and shot at swans, snipe, ducks, geese, deer, and alligators—most of which they failed to retrieve. Many of the waterfowl fell into dense reeds where our rugged outdoorsmen declined to venture because of mosquitoes. On their best day, the hunters shot eighty ducks, four geese, and two swans from stands situated at the edge of the reeds.

One of the members of the party summed up the adventure in a book called *Our Indian Summer in the Far West*: "Our bag for 10 days—on many of which we merely sailed or very successfully fished—amounted to 251 ducks, 12 geese, 5 swans, a few snipe, and an alligator. With retrievers we might have brought home at least 600 head of game; but we had more than we wanted, as after three days the birds were never eatable, and barely so in two."

By the turn of the century, the foreign nimrods (with considerable help from market hunters) had decimated game populations all over the West, and abandoned North America for fresh territory—Africa.

CAMELS IN TEXAS

"Our manifest destiny is to overspread the continent allotted by Providence for the free development of our yearly multiplying millions," read an early article in *United States Magazine and Democratic Review*.

Such ideals launched many schemes aimed at traversing the arid regions of the American West. One such plan in 1856 resulted in the importation of camels to Texas by the U.S. Army for experimental purposes. The idea came from U.S. Secretary of War Jefferson Davis.

Uncle Sam's unique herd found a permanent home at Camp Verde, sixty miles northwest of San Antonio. From there the camels proved their effectiveness on expeditions to the Big Bend area and to southern California. They also exhibited one major drawback. The didn't get along with the standard means of four-legged transportation of the day.

As one traveler noted: "The chief objection to using camels as beasts of burden in Texas is that horses usually run away at the sight of them. This is bad for the horses and worse for the pilot of the camel if the owner of the horses should have his pistol with him."

A camel among horses created such a hazard that the city of Brownsville enacted an ordinance banning the imported quadrupeds from the streets.

The Confederate army captured the Camel Brigade at the onset of the Civil War. The rebels, ironically, had much less admiration for the animals even though Jeff Davis originated the camel project. One rebel soldier stabbed a stubborn camel to death with his knife. Another group of Confederates shoved one over a bluff.

The Civil War and the transcontinental railroads brought an end to the camel experiment. The "ships of the desert" ultimately had little impact on the development of the West. The beasts ended up in circuses or in private hands. At least two were captured by Indians. Some of them simply wandered in the wilderness, bringing surprise to any humans whose paths they crossed.

A circuit preacher once delivered a sermon under a brush arbor near Camp Verde. As he read the Scripture from Mathew 23:24—"Ye blind guides, which strain at a gnat and swallow a camel"—he became suddenly speechless and stared beyond the congregation as if transfixed by some holy apparition. The church-goers turned to witness two camels emerging from the nearby woods.

Shortly after the Civil War, several men snuck through a thick morning fog on a "chicken stealing expedition." Suddenly, a giant goulish figure loomed on the trail ahead and descended upon the chicken thieves. The men panicked and fired their guns through the morning mist. They soon realized that their slain "devil-ghost" was only a camel with a U.S. brand. Such was the less-than-glorious death of the Camel Brigade.

THE PASSENGER PIGEON

They darkened the sky—literally shut out the sun with their wings. They could make a grove of trees look like the site of an artillery battle. They came in numbers that awed even men who had seen huge herds of buffalo cover the ground. It is undoubtable that the passenger pigeon was the most numerous species of birdlife the planet has ever hosted. Now they are all gone.

The "wild pigeons," as the settlers called them, came to Texas every year in the fall and stayed until about the end of February. They arrived in immense flocks that looked like huge dark rivers in the sky, a mile wide or wider. Though the birds flew fast enough to earn the nickname "Blue Meteors," some solid flocks took as long as fourteen hours to pass.

Frank Wilden said the pigeons sometimes flew too high to shoot with shotguns, but they flew so thick that a rifle aimed at a flock could never miss a bird. Skies so darkened when the pigeons arrived that domestic chickens went to roost, thinking dusk had fallen. Audubon estimated the population of a single flock at over a billion birds.

The individual birds resembled large versions of the mourning dove and were very tasty if not too old. This palatability and the passenger pigeon's instinct to do everything—nest, migrate, roost, feed—in huge numbers led to its downfall.

The southern range of the passenger pigeon covered the eastern half of Texas. The great plains represented their natural barrier to the west. Their roosts extended as far west in Texas as Lampasas and Uvalde. Descriptions of passenger pigeon roosts seem wildly exaggerated but numerous sources confirm them as true.

The birds roosted in thick woods or swamps, landing on every available inch of the tree branches, on every twig, and finally on the backs of other birds, three deep. Branches, huge limbs, even entire trees fell under the weight of pigeons. H.G. Askew saw a pigeon roost in 1855 in Wood County that was at least a square mile in area. Trees and limbs were crushed, broken, uprooted as if a tornado had ripped through.

The ground beneath such roosts was covered with dung in layers up to a foot deep or deeper. The pigeon guano produced amonia and nitrates in concentrations that could kill all vegetable life. However, old roosts, when cleared of dead trees and plowed, made extremely fertile farm land.

Early in the morning, the pigeons left their Texas roosts in huge flocks to feed on acorns, chestnuts, seeds, insects, and worms as far as 100 miles away. They burned energy quickly in the long, swift flights, so they gorged themselves with huge amounts of food. The pigeons wiped out acorn crops that settlers relied on to feed their hogs over the winter. In retribution, settlers killed hundreds of pigeons and fed them to the hogs.

Early farmers could shoot pigeons all day long and still not save fields just sewn with seed. The birds descended on the crop lands, the sound of their wings beating like a blizzard wind. Gunshots failed to scatter them for long. They just kept coming and eating.

In the evening, the birds returned from their feeding sites to their roosts in huge, dark clouds that some said looked like blue northers rolling in. Settlers from the surrounding areas gathered to harvest them by the thousands. C.V. Terrell and three other young men hunted a pigeon roost near Decatur in 1870. After dark, they loaded shotguns and carried lanterns into the roost to blind the birds, then began systematically blasting them from the branches.

They soon found they could save their ammunition and simply knock the heads off the birds with limbs they cut and stripped for the purpose. They killed more birds than they could use, giving the remainder to neighbors.

Other settlers burned sulphur under the roosts. The fumes caused the birds to drop by the hundreds. Settlers descended on the roosts at night and killed enough birds to fill sacks, barrels, wagons—seemingly without making a dent in the population. The following day they plucked and cleaned the birds, then salted or pickled them for future use.

Texans persecuted their share of passenger pigeons, but the real destruction of the species came at the hands of market hunters in the main nesting grounds north of the Ohio River from Wisconsin to New Hampshire. After 1850 the railroads made it easy for hunters to get the birds to market in the cities, and the devastation accelerated.

The pigeons left the South in February and established nesting colonies even larger than their southern roosts. A typical nesting colony was ten miles long and three miles wide with as many as 100 nests in every tree. The males and females paired off, cooperated in building their nest, and generally produced just one egg. The work of both parents was needed to incubate and feed the offspring. Hunters shot and netted the adults near the nesting areas by the hundreds of thousands. Every adult killed virtually ensured the death of a squab.

The adults that survived fattened their offspring then abandoned them, all the adults leaving the nesting areas on the same day. The squabs stayed in the nests for a day, then jumped to the ground where they wandered around for about three days until they learned to fly. During these three or four days, the fat little delicacies had no protection from the market hunters. Squab hunters slogged through the bird excrement as soon as the parents left in huge clouds. They used poles to punch the squabs from the nests, or they shook them out of trees or even burned them out.

Or they waited until the squabs bailed out and then simply picked them up by the bushels. Then hogs were brought in to feed on the dead birds left behind.

The young that survived were still pursued as they flew about in large flocks looking for food. Where they flew low, they could be taken with rocks, sticks, or clubs thrown into the air. Long poles were set in the ground and waved violently in the sky as the birds passed, knocking down scores of them. Both barrels of a 10-gauge shotgun could bring down seventy or more at a blast. Grape shot was fired from cannons. All manner of box traps and nets were designed to catch the birds alive so they could be fattened for market. One pigeoner soaked grain in alcohol and simply picked up the drunken birds. At night, on roost, the pigeons could be caught with bare hands.

Even as nesting colonies dwindled, the market hunters exploited them into oblivion. The birds did not learn to disperse for protection; the last wild specimens still banded together, making them easy to find and kill. The clouds of pigeons ceased to flow across our skies. A few pigeons in captivity failed to perpetuate the species. The passenger pigeon, once Earth's most highly populous bird species, reached the other extreme—extinction.

C.V. Terrell, who once knocked pigeons from a roost with a stick, seemed to miss the rivers of birds that quit coming to Texas. "We should have preserved and protected them as we have so wisely and effectively done and are now doing with all living wild life," he remarked. "With the wild pigeon we utterly failed."

THE MURDEROUS MEXICAN HOG

Just how mean is the javelina?

Texas folklore is full of stories of attacks by this animal, technically known as a peccary, and sometimes called a Mexican hog. Early Texas hunters had little fear of bears or lions but, as one of them remarked, "We gave the javelinas a wide berth."

Bigfoot Wallace called them "the most dangerous of all our wild animals." Once, while on a "scout" after Lipan Apaches, Bigfoot allowed a would-be novelist to ride with his ranger company. The author wanted some experience on the frontier so he could write with authenticity his proposed novel entitled *The Wayworn Wanderer of the Western Wilds*.

The author had a knack for getting into trouble, especially when he got himself "treed" by a pack of "Mexican hogs." Bigfoot heard him hollering for help and, at length, went to determine the novelist's plight more out of curiosity than concern. When Bigfoot saw the javelinas he also climbed a tree. The author was perched atop a thorn bush, drawing his legs toward his body to keep them out of reach of the peccaries.

"They look to me," said the novelist, referring to the javelinas, "like a couple of butcher knives about as long as my arm, stuck into a handle covered with hair and bristles!"

The ranger, stretched comfortably across a tree limb, passed the time telling stories that the novelist might be able to use in his book. He had only one bullet in his rifle and could not possibly frighten away the enraged javelinas.

Meanwhile, a vicious boar bit off the heel of the writer's boot. Another ripped away his pants leg and grazed his skin. Thorns stuck the author everywhere, and finally the javelinas began to gnaw his bush down.

"Captain," implored the doomed author, "you will find the manuscript of the 'Wayworn Wanderer' in my saddle bags. Take it and publish it for the benefit of the world. . . But tell them, for mercy's sake, that I was devoured by a lion, or a panther, or a catamount, or some decent sort of beast, and not by a gang of squealing pigs. It won't sound romantic, you know."

The ranger company showed up and dispatched the peccaries just as the author prepared to dive in among them.

Professional hunter Frank Wilden got into a similar scrape with Mexican hogs during a "settlement hunt." In the early days of Texas, small towns, or settlements, often challenged each other to hunting contests. The men of each town would take to the field for a day to see which settlement could shoot the most game. Squirrels and rabbits were worth one point a head while a turkey counted for five and a deer for ten. Rifles only were allowed.

Wilden joined in on a settlement hunt between two Brazos River communities. He and a teammate made a general run on squirrels (seventy head), rabbits (five) and turkey (one hen) before lunch. After lunching on barbecued rabbit, they saw something dark moving in a patch of sunflowers. When one of the hunters fired, a large herd of javelinas charged, grunting, squealing, and popping their teeth.

The teammates climbed separate trees and carried plenty of ammunition up with them. They couldn't afford to wait until the peccaries went away, losing valuable hunting hours for their team, so they effected a barrage from their tree limbs and killed thirty-two javelinas in the course of two hours.

Javelinas, considered inedible by early Texans, had a point value of zero in the settlement hunt. But when Wilden and his partner told their story of being treed, they were allowed thirty-two extra points which helped their town win the hunting contest. In all, Wilden claimed, 3,470 head of game were killed by both sides. The losers had to pay for "all the fluids consumed by the whole population of both places." The wild game feast started that evening, continued through the next day, and finally ended on the third morning of the gathering.

Meanwhile, out in the woods, the carcasses of thirty-two murderous javelina hogs provided an equal feast "for the vultures and wolves."

BOW-FISHING THROUGH THE AGES

Bow-fishing in Texas started way beyond the reach of the history books. The Karankawa Indians of the Gulf Coast were possibly the first Texas bow-fishermen.

Karankawa bowmen were not rapid-fire artists like the plains tribesmen, but their bows stunned with sheer power. The length of each brave's cedar bow, when strung, matched his height exactly. None but a "Kronk" could draw one. They could hit game at 100 yards. Their arrows could rip right through the body of a full-grown black bear and keep flying.

For their three-foot-long arrow shafts, the Kronks used bamboo-like cane. They fitted a small shaft of wood into each end of the cane. On one piece of wood they attached three feathers and carved a notch to fit their bowstring of twisted deer sinew. On the other piece of wood, they attached the arrowhead with deer sinews or asphaltum. Asphaltum is a black, tar-like substance that washes up in clumps along the coast.

Historians speculate that Karankawas developed extremely powerful bows to propel their arrows into the water while bow-fishing. This was their only means of fishing besides some cane fish traps they sometimes used. They fished from dugout canoes propelled by poles in the shallow flats, usually on the inland side of the coastal islands. The canoes were awkward vessels made of hollowed logs. The Kronks didn't even bother to remove the tree bark.

The Coahuiltecan tribesmen also shot fish with arrows. They hunted from the banks of rivers in South Texas. They added a new dimension to the sport by using torch lights to attract the fish at night.

A few white settlers also shot fish with bow and arrow, probably learning the methods from Indians. One old settler claimed his "Uncle Zac" had invented the sport: "Old Uncle Zac know'd fishes amazin' and, bein' naturally a hunter, he went to shootin' 'em with a bow and arrer to keep up early times in his history when he took Injuns and other varmints in the same way."

The fellow who recorded that quote was Frank Wilden, an adventurer who made his way through Texas hunting and fishing in early days. Wilden said "arrow-fishermen" in Texas used Indian dugout canoes or skiffs to shoot from. They used cedar bows and shot ash arrows. For weight, they used an iron arrow point eight inches long with a barb to keep it from pulling out of the fish. The arrow point slipped over the shaft and was not firmly attached. A twenty-foot length of cord, "about the size of a crow-quill," was attached to the iron point.

The arrow-fisherman tied the cord to the wrist of his bow arm and wrapped it around his forefinger so it would uncoil as the arrow flew. Carp and other rough fish were shot for the table. Alligator gars—measuring up to fifteen feet—were killed for sport. These monsters could tow a boat for up to an hour before growing tired enough to hoist to the surface for the kill.

Wilden claimed early bow-fishermen located feeding fish by bubbles and could determine the species of the fish by looking at the bubbles. They also listened for noises the fish made in the early spring. In May and June, fish came to the surface. Where a river entered a lake, fish could be shot "on the fly" as they swam near the surface.

One man paddled the boat while another shot fish. When the bubbles of a "feed" were spotted, the boatman paddled near. If the fish were too deep to see, the arrow-fisherman tapped the bottom of the boat with the back of his arrow to make the curious fish rise into view. When shot, the arrow shaft would separate from the iron point and float to the surface, to be retrieved for the next shot. The archer learned to aim deep to compensate for "the curious refractions of water."

It is only natural that "arrow-fishing" should find its way into Texas lore, and what better setting than mysterious Caddo Lake on the Texas-Louisiana border. In antebellum days, large plantations graced the shores of Caddo Lake. Wealthy Southern planters were some of the most avid outdoor sportsmen the world has ever known and must have practiced arrow-fishing from time to time, along with other forms of hunting and fishing.

The vessel of choice on Caddo Lake in those days was the bateau—sort of a cross between a canoe and a pirouge. A Caddo Lake planter named Jackson, so the story goes, never went out in his bateau without his bow and fishing arrow at his feet. Jackson loved arrow-fishing, specializing in landing huge alligator gar.

However, Jackson was most well known among lake settlers for another eccentricity. He had an obsession for discovering the secret of perpetual motion. With mechanical genius, he invented odd contraptions that he hoped would give the world a never-ending source of free energy.

Jackson paddled his bateau across the lake to Port Caddo one day to fetch materials from the blacksmith for one of his perpetual motion machines. While paddling home, he crossed paths with a monster alligator gar, rolling on the surface. The fish was longer than his sixteen-foot bateau! He shot his fishing arrow on impulse, tied the line off to the front of his bateau, and soon found the little boat curling back the lake's surface behind the deep-swimming gar.

At length, Jackson leaned back in his craft and enjoyed the ride, for the gar was pulling straight for his plantation on the north shore. Then he saw that more good fortune awaited him. Several of his friends had come to visit and were waiting on the bluff over the lake for his return. Jackson would need their help to land the trophy gar.

He waved for assistance. His friends waved back but launched not a single craft to come to his aid. Jackson shouted. His friends cheered unintelligibly from the bluff. Jackson threw his hat aloft in frustration. His friends also launched their headgear and jumped up and down as if celebrating his predicament.

The gar pulled Jackson all the way to the Louisiana line. Finally, he cut the fishing cord with his pocket knife and paddled home, arriving well after dark.

Furious now, Jackson demanded a satisfactory explanation from his friends. Why hadn't they come to his aid in landing the gar? "Gar?" they replied with disappointment. They thought for certain, having seen Jackson skim effortlessly across the lake, that he had at long last unlocked the perplexing mysteries of perpetual motion!

SNAKE STORIES

Texas tradition with rattlers goes back as far as the days of the first explorers. Of course, just as the Texas blue norther was colder back then, the Texas rattler was bigger, meaner, and even had the power to enchant its victims.

In 1846 a French adventurer visited Texas and later recorded his observations in a book. In it, he described the killing of a monster rattlesnake in what is now Medina County. A "tiger hunter," the Frenchman said, had sat down to rest on what he thought was the trunk of a fallen tree when he discovered that it was actually the body of a huge rattlesnake. Of course the hunter killed the rattler and "the reptile measured seventeen feet in length, eighteen inches in circumference, and had twenty-five rings or rattles."

Perhaps the foreigner stretched that snake substantially before measuring it, although the *Dallas Morning News* of July 28, 1877 reported the killing of an eighteen-footer with thirty-seven rattles in Indian Territory.

Tradition has it that early settlers of the lower Colorado River killed a ten-foot rattlesnake with fifty rattles. A cotton farmer near Packsaddle Mountain in Llano County supposedly killed a rattler measuring ten feet, four inches. A San Antonio stagecoach once had to stop to kill an eight-plus-footer "as large around the body as the leg of a good-sized man."

A cowboy down in the Rio Grande Valley shot two monster snakes that had killed a steer. One measured ten feet, three inches; the other nine feet, eight inches. The skins of these two monsters hung in a Harlingen drugstore for many years.

Sometime during Texas' colonial days, two neighbors—
James McKenzie and Andrew Northington—went hunting
along the Colorado River in what is now Wharton County.
A sudden storm blew in and prompted the two men to squat
against the downwind side of a pair of big trees for shelter
from the wind and rain. When the storm passed, James McKenzie rose from his
position against his tree only to discover that he had all the
while been sitting on a coiled rattlesnake. As McKenzie
rose, the snake bit him "on the under part of the thigh."

Andrew Northington, a true friend, killed the snake,
scarified the wound, and sucked the blood and poison from
it. The victim "suffered no serious inconvenience."

In the 1870s a fellow who made his living selling whiskey
to buffalo hunters of the North Texas plains won the nickname of "Snakehead" Thompson. This entrepreneur knew
that his clientele enjoyed potent libations, so in each barrel
of whiskey he sold to the hunters, he included one or two
rattlesnake heads for extra flavor.

Many Texas pioneers claimed that rattlesnakes had the
ability to charm or hypnotize their prey. Supposedly, any
critter—human or otherwise—that stared into the beady
eyes of a rattler could escape the trance only through lucky
intervention of some outside source.

J. Frank Dobie, in his definitive book on rattler lore entitled *Rattlesnakes*, told of his own experience with an
almost hypnotizing rattler. Dobie was stalking through a
shallow gully after a whitetail buck when he heard the
warning rattles just ahead. "The hair of my head began to
rise; cold shivers ran down my back; the entire surface of
my body became gooseflesh." But the big snake was not en-
chanting enough to completely paralyze Dobie. He instantly
forgot about deer hunting, raised his 30-30, and killed the
over-six-footer.

'GATOR TALES

Alligators are off the endangered species list now in Texas and inhabit parts of ninety counties. In some places they have even been called nuisances. They found their place in Texas lore long ago.

When the French explorer La Salle crossed the Brazos River in 1687—before the river had a name—he called that stream *la Maligne* on account of an alligator. *La Maligne* means "mischievous" in French. La Salle so named the river because a 'gator ate one of his servants who was swimming across. LaSalle had strange ideas about what constituted mere mischief. Maybe that's why his men mutinied and killed him a month later.

The Karankawa Indians, cannibals of the Texas Coast, had a fondness for alligator meat as well as certain other delicacies. Mary Helm lived on the coast in Karankawa country in the 1830s. She wrote the following about "Kronks" and 'gators.

"Alligator meat is a great luxury with them, and although supplied bountifully with fresh meat, they would be absent frequently and return with pieces of cooked alligator tied between large pieces of bark swung over their shoulders. I have seen them killed. The creature is helpless when under the water and the Indians dive and stick him with a sharp knife."

After the Alamo fell, many Texas citizens began a haphazard retreat toward the United States known as the "Runaway Scrape." Many of them died from disease and exposure. An alligator killed one man. He swam his horses across a bayou then swam back to help his family across.

The water was up and the family talked him out of crossing just then, so he had to swim back over and get his horses. An alligator attacked him before he reached his horses. The 'gator struck the victim with its tail and then pulled him under. A few days later, some men who had witnessed the attack used a quarter of beef as bait to lure the man-eater out and then shot it to death.

An unknown author made a trip through Texas during colonial days and wrote a book about his adventures called *A Visit to Texas*. He captured a two-foot 'gator by throwing a noose around its head. He drug the little reptile to the home of a Texan who owned a pet bear. When the young alligator went after the full-grown black bear, the bruin hastily climbed a tree.

The same unknown author discovered a huge sixteen-foot alligator on the Trinity River. After shooting sixteen rifle balls into the animal, the Texas visitor got tired of wasting lead and tied the 'gator to a log. The next morning he returned, expecting to find a dead alligator. He found a broken rope instead.

Jim Bowie used to ride alligators in Louisiana. His technique involved jumping on a 'gator's back, gouging thumbs into the eyes to obscure its vision, and pulling up on the upper jaw with his fingers to keep the amphibian from diving.

Another Louisiana product who rode 'gators for fun was Ben Lilly. Lilly could coax 'gators within rifle range by imitating the whine of a puppy. Some 'gator hunters used real dogs to lure specimens closer. A good 'gator dog would fetch any stick thrown into the water yet stay just a few strokes ahead of approaching alligators.

Ben Lilly had an affinity for one particular alligator in Louisiana named Old Lep. Lilly often poled a skiff into Old Lep's cypress swamp and poked the giant 'gator with the pole just to make Old Lep roar. One day Lilly found Old Lep on the shore and lassoed him for sport. The big bull 'gator surprised Lilly by rolling over the ground, quickly taking the slack out of the rope. Lilly's hand got tangled and the brute began to reel him in. Lilly managed to grab his rifle, poke it into Old Lep's mouth, and shoot the bull to death.

Buffalo Bayou once held an abundance of alligators. The Allen brothers plotted the townsite of Houston along the bayou in 1836. A party of young fellows decided to go find this new city. They searched for a long time in the piney woods, and when they found Houston, it consisted of "one dugout canoe, a bottle gourd of whiskey, and a surveyor's chain and compass and was inhabited by four men with an ordinary camping outfit." They also found mosquitoes the size of grasshoppers and decided to take a dip in Buffalo Bayou to fend off the insects.

They dove into the clear, cool water and had a nice swim for a few minutes. Then a swarm of alligators showed up and made the grasshopper-sized mosquitoes appear altogether harmless. The men vacated the bayou immediately; one of them had to swim to the far shore where he saw a large panther creeping toward him through the underbrush. His friends rescued him in the only dugout canoe the city of Houston possessed at the time.

When steamboats began serving Houston, passengers made sport of shooting alligators along the banks of Buffalo Bayou from the decks of the paddle-wheelers, much like railroad passengers slaughtered buffalo from the windows of train cars on the western plains.

Unlike the buffalo, however, the alligator has made a comeback in Texas, thanks to conservation and resource management. Texas 'gator stories—part of our lore since the time of La Salle—will surely continue to surface.

MULE ARTILLERY

"Dragging cannons here and there over the Plains in pursuit of hostile Indians," claimed army scout Billy Dixon, "was about as feasible as hitting a hummingbird with a brickbat." It seems that rugged country in the frontier West simply defied the use of wheel-mounted artillery to combat Indians.

More than one frontiersman, however, tried an alternative to gun carriages that might have revolutionized the tactics of frontier warfare . . . if it had only worked. The alternative was the mule.

Probably the first innovator in the field of mule artillery was Don Martin de Leon, the Spanish empresario and founder of Victoria, Texas. It was 1806 and Comanches had stolen several beeves from de Leon's Aransas River ranch. So de Leon had one of his vaqueros assist him in cinching his ancient Spanish "thunder gun" onto the back of a mule. He loaded the cannon himself with an extra charge of powder and a handful of scrap iron.

Martin de Leon planned to fire the cannon from the ground, but when he and his vaquero encountered an unexpected Comanche scouting party, the vaquero panicked and lit the fuse while the big gun was still on the mule's back. The poor beast died with a broken back from the recoil.

By the time the early Texas settler and writer Noah Smithwick came through Victoria in 1828, the story of de Leon and his mule artillery had branched out quite a bit. The version Smithwick heard and recorded in his book *Evolution of a State* said de Leon mounted a "jackass" with a "four-pounder swivel gun," organized his servants and vaqueros into an army, and set out to annihilate the entire Karankawa tribe.

But de Leon, according to Smithwick, forgot to "brace up" the jackass before he fired the swivel gun at the enemy. The recoil somersaulted the beast, landing him on top of the cannon with his feet in the air. Thus fixed, the jackass refused to move until released from the artillery.

During the Civil War, a remarkable Confederate soldier named John R. Baylor (who had been busted from the rank of colonel to private but would later become a general) experimented with equine artillery. Salvaging parts from captured U.S. warships, he devised a method of carrying light cannon into battle on the backs of mules.

Henry W. Strong, in *My Frontier Days and Indian Fights on the Plains*, described General Nelson A. Miles' use of mule artillery against Indians in 1874 at Tule Canyon, in West Texas. "He shelled them from the north side of the canyon with a mountain howitzer which was carried on a pack mule. He could do no damage."

Next comes the tale written by a nineteenth-century humorist who called himself John Phoenix, the pseudonym and alter ego of George H. Derby, Lt., U.S. Army. Derby graduated West Point in 1846. After surviving wounds in the war with Mexico, he explored the lower Colorado River, Southern California, and the virgin forests of the Great Northwest. He built government roads and dams from San Diego to Vancouver. But in his spare time, Lt. Derby, under the pen name of John Phoenix, recorded the humor of the West in witty articles published by newspapers and magazines from San Francisco to New York.

For some reason, Phoenix didn't mention the names of the principles who tested the experimental alternative to spoke-wheeled gun carriages, and he didn't say at which particular fort the testing took place. Perhaps he swore to protect the identities of those involved from the embarrassment that ensued. He did note that "no report of the results of the experiment was ever sent to the War Department."

Anyway, the major out in John Phoenix's western fort had found his artillery extremely difficult to transport over rugged country, so he began to improvise. All the officers of the post joined in on the experiment with great interest. The commandant rigged a pack saddle to accommodate a howitzer cannon. The adjutant helped strap the experimental contraption to the post's most docile ambulance mule. The lieutenants led a detail down the nearby bluff to set up a target at the riverbank.

The anxious officers finally led their steadfast beast of burden to the bluff, backed the quadruped up to the edge of the precipice, and positioned the muzzle of the howitzer to bear over the animal's rump. The major loaded the cannon with a ball cartridge, dropped a time fuse in the touch hole, and held a match flame to it.

The officers stood around the front of the mule in a semicircle, awaiting the outcome of the shot. But the stoic old ambulance mule became annoyed at the fizzing on his back and craned his neck to determine the source. Unable to find it, he turned, causing the howitzer to sweep around the horizon and point into the panic-stricken face of each successive officer in the semicircle. The mule became so vexed that he continued in his whirling mode, making a revolution every ten seconds.

The commandant climbed a tree. The lieutenants sprang over the bluff. The adjutant sprinted for the fort. The major simply rolled to the ground with a groan.

At last the howitzer roared. The recoil lifted the mule, rump-first, into a somersaulting plunge down the bluff where he landed at the bottom of the river. The cannon ball whistled off toward the fort, struck the chimney of the major's quarters, knocked some bricks into the parlor, and so frightened the major's wife that she suffered convulsions.

At any rate, the use of mule artillery never became wide-spread, and cannon continued to be largely ineffective against hard-riding Indians. Frederick Law Olmstead, the landscape architect and frontier traveler, saw six-pounders in use during the Indian wars and was moved to remark that "keeping a bulldog to chase mosquitoes would be of no greater nonsense."

PART 5

WILDEST TALES

HAIR OF THE FISH

Wilbur Foshay recognized a good public relations stunt when he saw one. In November of 1938 a fisherman from Pratt, Kansas, sent a brief directive to Foshay's office at the Salida, Colorado, Chamber of Commerce:

"Answer collect by Western Union if you have fur-bearing trout in Arkansas River there."

As secretary of the Chamber of Commerce, Foshay had heard stories of the Arkansas's hairy fish before, but it took the letter from Kansas to set him off. He immediately went to work promoting the regional curiosity. He even found a local photographer who had a convincing photo of the underwater wonder. Foshay sent a copy of the picture to the curious Kansas fisherman, then called the newspapers.

The Pueblo *Chieftain* picked up the story and decided to investigate further. It ran quotes from several "real old-timers" along the upper Arkansas who remembered seeing fur-bearing trout in large numbers years before. However, when it came to explaining the current scarcity of the trout, the old-timers could not agree.

"Narrow-Gauge Ned of Poncha Pass" told the *Chieftain* his pappy had once kept some fur-bearing trout over at the hot springs. But over several generations the steam ruined the fur, and the species finally left to seek cooler waters.

"Texas Creek Tess" said fox raisers had killed off the trout to keep them from cross-breeding with the foxes and corrupting the pure bloodlines that produced fine fur coats.

"Harrison Hickoryhead, the Gorgemore graybeard," said eastern capitalists had trapped the trout into near extinction. "There's still some of 'em around if you know where to look, which I do, but I ain't tellin'," the *Chieftain* quoted him as saying.

The article in the *Chieftain* only encouraged Wilbur Foshay. He obtained a special license from the state game and fish commission allowing him to set a trap line for the pelted fish. The Alamosa *Courier* reported that Foshay's trappers managed to catch three muskrats but no fur-bearing trout.

The Lamar *Daily News* soon ran a story saying Wilbur Foshay had three mounted fur-bearing trout on display at his chamber of commerce office but added that the pelts looked suspiciously like muskrat skins. "They were splendid examples of taxidermy," the report said.

The *Daily News* then suggested that Arkansas River trout collected a fungus in the winter that many anglers had merely mistaken for fur. This claim was challenged by another fine news organ, however. The Elk Mountain *Pilot* had done some research, and finally published its own version of the origin of the species. According to the *Pilot*, the story began at Leadville, near the source of the Arkansas River, in 1877.

The silver boom erupted in Leadville that year, and miners streamed in from everywhere. That first winter, the only fare available was venison and fried potatoes. The miners ate so much of the stuff that venison tallow became caked in the roofs of their mouths. The tallow got so thick they couldn't taste their beverages. Miners were voracious consumers of beverages, so something had to be done.

Finally a desperate pick-axe man wired a pile of pitch splinters to the top of his head and set it on fire. The heat from the blaze penetrated his skull, and what little brains he had, and melted the tallow in the roof of his mouth so he could once again enjoy the flavors of his favorite drinks. Before long every miner in camp was using the same method. There was just one drawback. About ninety-seven percent of the men in Leadville went bald.

In the spring of 1878 a fellow from Kentucky arrived with a cure for baldness that he manufactured from potatoes. He found a perfect place to make his tonic near a small creek south of Leadville.

One rainy evening the tonic maker was delivering four jugs of his remedy for baldness to Leadville. He had to cross the creek on a foot log. He slipped on the rain-slick timber and dropped two of the jugs. They broke open on some rocks and the hair tonic washed downstream into the Arkansas River.

Soon, fur-bearing trout were being caught by the creel. But the best fishing method differed from the standard fly rod technique. According to the *Pilot*, the most successful anglers would "stick a red, white, and blue pole into the bank, put on a white coat, wave a copy of the *Police Gazette* in one hand and brandish a scissors in the other, and yell, 'Next,' until they had the limit of these fine fur-bearing trout with full beards, etc. The trout would leap up onto the bank. . ."

To prove the Arkansas indeed bore piscatorial pelts, Wilbur Foshay had done everything short of outright lying. Like any good publicist, he knew the newspapers would take over from there.

SAVE THE JACKALOPE

Once, a stranger couldn't enter Palo Duro Canyon, in the Texas Panhandle, without feeling a certain dread of the whang-doodle; or trek the virgin forests of the Great Northwest without fearing an agrapelter ambush; or drink at a Mojave Desert water hole without keeping a nervous eye trained for the carnivorous carvana.

Mythical animals like the whang-doodle, the agrapelter, and the carvana used to swarm across the West in great numbers. But these days only one timid species continues to thrive. Looking exactly like a jackrabbit, except for the antlers protruding from its head, it goes by the name of jackalope. Mounted specimens are common in trophy rooms across the West, but to spot one in the wild you have to have keen eyesight, quick feet, and a vivid imagination. Part hare, part deer, the jackalope represents the consummation of a long-standing Western tradition—the creation of fictional fauna.

The tradition began back when explorers were still charting trackless regions of the North American continent. The New World had already produced flying squirrels, horned toads, and snakes with rattles on their tales. As frontiersmen pushed westward, more strange beasts appeared. Folks back East were dying to hear what odd creature would turn up next, and Westerners simply didn't want to disappoint them. If they couldn't find any new species, they just had to make them up.

Don Biggers, editor of a Texas newspaper called the *Rotan Billy Goat*, ran several stories about the depredations of a wildcat/badger/lobo wolf hybrid called the wampus cat. The local folks were all in on the hoax, but visitors to the upper Brazos River region often left Rotan dreading an encounter with the vicious beast they had read about in the local rag.

Greenhorns heard warnings about other dangerous monsters in towns all across the West. One particularly dangerous species was the terrible carvana. No one could describe this beast, for it lived underwater and had never been seen. But it had dragged many thirsty travelers to the depths as they stooped to drink at springs, ponds, or rivers.

In timbered country, people had to keep a constant watch for the carcajou. This panther-like blood-sucker had a prehensile tail that gripped with the strength of a boa constrictor. It would drop on its victims from tree limbs, enwrap them with its tail, and tap into the handiest jugular vein.

Timbermen of the Great Northwest woods uttered warnings of another sylvan ambusher. The agrapelter was known to pounce on lumberjacks and pummel them senseless with a billet-like tail.

An even more unusual tail belonged to the glyptodont, also called the whang-doodle, a denizen of Texas' Palo Duro Canyon. The glyptodont looked like a huge kangaroo with a wide, rubbery tail. This appendage allowed the animal to jump from the canyon rim and still effect a soft landing. It also used its tail in swatting boulders across the canyon to bombard invading humans.

Certain mountain ranges in the West hosted an unusual alpine curiosity. Some described it as a cross between a buffalo and a mountain goat. Others claimed it looked something like a mule. It was known variously as the gwinter, side-swiper, prock, mountain stem-winder, side-hill saugus, and binder.

Because it lived its entire life on the slopes, the legs of the stem-winder were shorter on one side than the other. There were two subspecies of stem-winders endemic to some locales. The counterclockwise breed had its short legs on the left side. The clockwise variety's right legs were shorter. With both, the short-legged side always had to face uphill. When a clockwise stem-winder encountered a counterclockwise stem-winder on a mountain slope, a fight to the death ensued, for neither beast could turn to retreat. On some peaks one subspecies totally wiped out the other.

Talk of stem-winders and whang-doodles made some gullible dudes ask to see the alleged creatures. To avoid disappointing the tourists, Westerners had to convince strangers that the pseudo-species possessed such remarkable escape abilities that they were almost impossible to locate. A sorrowful animal called the squank, for example, washed its tracks away by crying constantly.

Another elusive animal was known as the hide-behind bird. Hunters often found its tracks on the ground where it had been standing right behind them just seconds before. But when they turned quickly for a look, the bird always moved too fast to allow a glimpse, remaining behind the hunter, no matter how quickly he twisted. And even when the best of trackers tried to trail the hide-behind bird, they failed.

The first Westerner to see a hide-behind bird accidentally sat on a cactus and, jumping straight up in the air, happened to look down between his boots. He then spotted the bird, and discovered why it had never been successfully trailed. Its feet grew out backwards. After that discovery the hide-behind birds were tracked down and hunted into extinction.

The milamo bird was a crypto-zoological species with a sense of humor. Smaller than an ostrich, larger than a crane, this bird bored for foot-long worms by shoving its auger-like beak into the ground, and walking around in a circle until it had screwed its entire neck into the dirt. When it found a worm, it would pull until the worm snapped out of the ground and popped the milamo bird in the eye. The milamo was a good sport, however, and always sat down to have a good laugh on itself—a laugh that could be heard a mile away.

Victims of the old animal hoaxes were wise to emulate the milamo bird. Anyone who has ever been duped into a snipe hunt knows that good sportsmanship and hearty laughter can soothe a bruised ego better than anything, with the possible exception of getting even.

But today, much of our mythical menagerie has gone the way of the hide-behind bird—reasoned into oblivion. Only the jackalope and a few others remain. There is always the hope, however, that new species will evolve. Their breeding grounds lie within the vivid and inventive Western imagination—one resource we may never exhaust.

"Git Up, Dan!"

Dan and Hattie were newlyweds in a ranch country. Dan knew horses. He'd spent so much time astraddle of them that he was starting to act like one himself in some respects. He'd take a deep breath and flap his lips whenever he felt contented. He could make his skin twitch when a fly landed on him. And when Dan got mad, you could almost see his ears lay back.

Things went well in Dan and Hattie's marriage for the first several months. Then one day, Hattie decided she wanted a garden. "Dan, hitch a mule and get out there and turn me over about an acre of sod," she said.

Dan stood there for a moment. He never had liked sod busting. He shook his head and stamped his hind foot. "I'd like to, Hattie," he answered, "but I've got fence to mend in the northwest pasture today. Maybe tomorrow."

The next day at breakfast, Hattie said, "Dan, are you gonna break that garden patch for me today like you said you would?"

Dan tossed his head and stared at her like a colt at a new gate. "Oh, Hattie, darlin', you know I'm itchin' to get around to that, but I've got that windmill to fix in the bull trap. Might take a couple of days."

A couple of days later, Hattie said, "The garden patch, Dan. It'll only take you a few hours."

"I know," he said, rubbing his rump on a fence post. "But the thing is, there's a big covey of quail lives in the high grass on that field, and I want to get the shotgun after 'em a couple of times before I plow all that grass under."

"I swear," Hattie snapped, "If you don't stop coming up with excuses and plow that garden for me tomorrow, I'm gonna put you in harness and make you pull that plow yourself!"

The next morning, Dan tried to saddle up after breakfast, but Hattie was ready for him. She threw a loop on him and snubbed him to a fence post. She tied one foot up until she could get the blinders and plow harness on him. Then she turned him toward the field she had chosen as her garden site and said, "Git up, Dan."

Hattie put the reins over her shoulder, took hold of the plow handles, and started turning grass upside down. Dan balked once, but she shook the reins and said, "Hup, there, Dan," and he lunged against the traces again.

They were almost to the end of the turn row, when that covey of quail flew up right under Dan's front feet. It was a boom year for quail, and this covey numbered two dozen if not a hundred. They came out of a circle formation and flew in every direction, some of them flying up under Dan's belly and bouncing off his flanks.

Now Dan had never been in harness before, so he was a little skittish anyhow, but when that covey took flight, he boogered something fierce and took off all wall-eyed and tail-high.

He jerked Hattie to the ground and swung wide back toward the house, the plow bouncing behind him, spooking him all the more. The dog barked at him when he ran past the woodpile, and he shied into the chicken coop, scattering the hens.

He blundered into the clothesline Hattie had made of binder twine, and pulled the whole mess of flapping bed sheets and long handles down on his back.

He circled the pasture in terror, then tried to jump the bobwire fence, but got the plow hung and pulled the staples out of a quarter mile of fence line before he finally hit the corner post and threw himself down.

Hattie came running up as Dan was thrashing in the harnesses. "Dan, have you lost your mind?" she said. "Don't you have sense enough to lay still when you get throwed down?"

"Me?" he shouted. "Woman, you don't even know enough to holler 'whoa!'"

The worst part of the whole deal was that Dan had to give up quail hunting. The next time he flushed a covey, it spooked him so bad that he bowed a tendon running away. He stayed lame so long Hattie thought she was going to have to swap him off.

THE WORLD'S SMARTEST HOUND

It was after midnight on the Busted Stirrup Ranch, down in the Colorado River bottoms. Old Jim White, Doc Jones, and Big Buddy Wilson—coon-huntin' rivals—sat around their campfire, waiting. Every now and then, one would stop whittling and turn his head to catch some sound drifting on the wind: maybe a bullfrog's croak, or a coyote's howl, or a hoot owl's hoot.

Finally they heard what they had been listening for. It echoed through the dark pecan bottoms like a rasp and a holler rolled together—the mournful music of a hound with the scent of a coon in his nostrils. As best they could tell, it came from Possum Prairie, about a mile east, upwind, across Peach Creek.

"'Bout time ol' Dodger found a trail," Big Buddy remarked. "I thought you said he was smart. A smart hound would have treed a coon by now."

Old Jim White shifted the chaw of tobacco in his cheek, spit in the fire, and smiled. "Ol' Dodger won't run just any coon," he said. "He's smarter than that. He waits for a big one. He's been over at Peach Creek all this time, sticking his tongue out to measure how deep them coon tracks mash down in the mud. Judges their weight that way. That Dodger's the world's smartest hound."

Big Buddy turned his head to listen to the dog sing in the night. "You oughtn't to claim that till I tell you about ol' Star," he said. "I woned him when I lived up in them Guadalupe River cedar brakes." He paused, cocked his head. From the sound of things, Dodger had run down into Peach Creek after his coon.

"Now, them Hill Country coons are the smartest in Texas," Big Buddy continued. "They'll find 'em a limestone bluff and run them dogs up and down it till they're plumb wore out and can't chase no more. But ol' Star was wise to that angle. He'd chase 'em up a bluff once, then just sit at the bottom and wait for 'em to come back down, and there he had 'em.

"Well, one day this fellow came out to the ranch with some high-bred hounds and wanted to run some coons with 'em. I told 'em ol' Star would show 'em how, and we turned 'em out. After Star had treed three or four coons—or maybe it was a dozen—this fellow told me to take Star back home and tie him up because his high-bred hounds wasn't gettin' no work in. So I tied Star to the barn door and we let them high-breds have one to theirself."

Big Buddy stopped to listen as Dodger turned south with a fresh moan in his voice.

"Well?" Old Jim asked. "Did them high-bred hounds get their coon or not?"

"Well, they tried," Buddy said, "but some old smart coon run 'em up and down every bluff in the county. Then the dangdest thing happened. It was near daylight and I heard ol' Star's voice in with the pack of high-breds. He had gotten loose and joined 'em. We rode across the divide to where we heard the dogs, and just at dawn that ol' coon come lopin' out of the cedar brakes, and there comes ol' Star right behind him. I had tied him to the barn door, you recall, but he had pulled the whole door off and was draggin' it. And those high-bred hounds—why, they wasn't so dumb after all. They was all ridin' on that barn door, just a-howlin' their lungs out!"

Doc Jones had been listening politely up until this time, but now he threw his whittling stick into the fire and glared at Big Buddy. "Buddy, you wouldn't know the truth if it poleaxed you between the eyes!"

"I swear it really happened!" Buddy insisted.

"Oh, I believe the part about the barn door, because I've seen it happen several times myself. But you're stretching the truth to say ol' Star was the smartest hound in the world. There's been a dang sight smarter than that! Just let me tell you about ol' Petunia. Now, there was the smartest dog ever to bark up a cold trail. Why, back in forty-three. . ."

Doc Jones suddenly stopped and cupped a hand behind his good ear. "Jim," he said, "I believe ol' Dodger has quit singin'. I thought you said that dog was smart, but he's gone and lost his trail!"

"No he hasn't," Old Jim answered, smiling confidently. "You just go on and tell us about this Petunia, and about the time you get through, Dodger will take to bayin' again. He's knows what he's doin'."

"Well, alright," Doc said, shrugging. "But you talk about a hound who knew what she was doin'—that was Petunia. Back in forty-three there was an old lobo lived down in the Brush Country, name of the graveyard wolf, on account of he'd always run a pack of hounds past this particular graveyard before he'd stretch out and hit the high places. A friend of mine finally told me to bring ol' Petunia down and get that wolf, so I did.

"Petunia didn't take no time findin' the trail. She dogged the graveyard wolf for four hours, until finally the ol' boy come by that graveyard, kicked into high gear, and left Petunia so far behind she had to warm the trail up with her breath before she could smell it.

"But, like I said, ol' Petunia was the smartest hound ever lived, and she got her an idea. She turned tail right there and back-trailed that lobo. Took her fifty-three hours to do it, but she back-trailed the graveyard wolf to when he was a pup and caught him before he even had his eyes open!"

Just then, ol' Dodger's voice opened up again across the bottoms, clearer and more joyful than ever before.

"He's found the trail again!" Big Buddy remarked.

"Never lost it," Old Jim said.

"Then how come him to stop singin' for that little spell back yonder?" Doc asked.

Old Jim spit into the fire and listened with satisfaction to the tobacco juice sizzle on an ember. "I told you ol' Dodger was the world's smartest hound. He was crossin' posted land!"

LYIN' DOGS AND LYIN' ABOUT 'EM

Any coon hunter worth his weight in pelts wants a smart dog, of course, but some old hunters say it's possible for dogs to get too smart. When they have trailed and treed coons often enough, they start thinking they can improve on the process. For coon dogs, the hunt works about the same way every time. First, the hunter lets them loose to hunt up a trail. Then they follow the trail until they jump the coon. Then they run the coon until it climbs a tree. Then they bay under the tree until the hunter comes along, shoots the coon, takes the dogs home, and gives them a well-deserved meal.

Well, some smart dogs get to thinking about this process and decide a few unnecessary steps might be alleviated. So they just skip the parts about finding a trail and chasing the coon. They go straight to the nearest tree, bay, and wait for the grub.

These kinds of dogs are referred to as "lying" coon dogs, and the hunter is apt to get rid of them pretty soon because he can't stand the competition. It's not for dogs to lie about coons, it's for hunters to lie about dogs.

One fellow, for example, owned a pointer that he claimed could find a bird no matter how carefully concealed. This fellow said he went to a saloon one day, and natually, he took his dog along because they were always together. When a stranger walked into the bar, the bird dog perked up, dashed over to the stranger, slid to a stop across the hardwood floor, and assumed the most perfect pointing stance ever seen. This startled the stranger a great deal, so the owner of the dog got up to apologize.

"I'm sorry my dog is acting that way, stranger," he said, "but he obviously smells a bird on you. Do you happen to have one in your pocket?"

"No," said the stranger.

"Well, have you handled a bird in the last few days or so?"

"No, I haven't."

"Have you shook hands with any bird hunters since the season opened?"

"I don't even know any bird hunters," said the stranger.

"Well, this is odd, then," said the dog's owner. "I hope my dog hasn't offended you, Mr. . .?"

"Partridge," said the stranger.

Other dogs become famous for their persistence in holding a point. Back when prairie chickens were numerous enough to provide Texas settlers with regular drumsticks, a certain hunter had a pointer that he claimed would hold a bird till doomsday. On one hunt this dog got into a field of tall gama grass and disappeared. The hunter knew the dog had set some chickens, but the grass was head high and he couldn't find the dog. He called but the dog wouldn't leave the birds.

Finally, the hunter went home, thinking the dog would get hungry sooner or later and return to the cabin, but he didn't show. About three days later, a prairie fire swept the entire region. The old settler went back to the burned off field and found his pointing dog holding a prairie chicken about thirty feet from him, both of them burned to a crisp.

Another dog owner liked to tell about his pet that was half water spaniel and half Walker hound. He took this dog with him one day on a fishing trip and let the dog sit in the front of the boat. After the fisherman had landed a bass and a catfish, the dog seemed to catch on to the idea of the sport and started looking down into the water. Suddenly, he barked once and jumped in. He stayed under for fifteen minutes and the fisherman thought his faithful friend had drowned. Then he heard the dog baying across the lake so he paddled to the shore where he found that the hound had treed eleven flathead catfish and nine largemouth bass.

The one type of dog probably most celebrated by dog owners is the "cold-nosed hound," one that can find and follow a "cold" trail. J. Frank Dobie wrote that the best of these hounds could "snuff the cobwebs out of some coon's trail, warm it up with their breath and follow it."

One fellow said his cold-nosed hound trailed a fresh coon track to a field that had just been plowed. The coon had passed in front of the tractor and the farmer had plowed the scent under so the dog couldn't follow. The farmer got in a good crop that year, and when he plowed his field again he turned the coon scent back up, and the dog picked up the trail from there and treed the coon in no time.

But there have been hounds with even colder noses. In *Tales of Old-Time Texas*, Dobie tells of the time Jim Borroum and Jeff Porter went hunting down on the San Antonio River. Porter turned loose his two hounds, Bowie and Bonham, and listened to the music the two of them made as they chased two different coons into the same thicket.

The hunters rode to the spot and found that the two coons, oddly enough, had climbed the same tree and it was a dead tree at that. Jim Borroum swore the dogs must be lying, for he had never known a coon to take to a dead tree for cover. But Jeff Porter said his dogs never lied, and there were definitely two coons in that tree. He climbed the tree, looked into a hollow at a fork of two big branches, and found two coon skeletons inside.

"This tree was not dead and them coons weren't dead neither when they clumb it," said Porter. "I told you Bowie and Bonham were the best cold-nosed hounds that ever worked a cold trail."

Not even a cold-nosed hound, however, can beat the story old Uncle Pie used to tell about his coon hound down on the Brazos River bottoms. Uncle Pie was chopping cord wood with a double-bladed axe down in the woodlot one day about sundown when the urge to go coon hunting struck him. He sunk one end of his double-bladed axe into a stump and left it there. Then he hiked back to his cabin to tell his hound, Zeke, that they were going hunting that night.

About midnight, Uncle Pie turned Zeke loose in the bottoms, and in no time the hound had a coon on the run. Uncle Pie listened for hours from a high point of land as Zeke ran the coon up and down the bottoms. Finally, he could tell that the coon was running through the woodlot, and all of a sudden Uncle Pie heard a yelp so horrible that it curdled his blood in his veins.

Running to the woodlot, he found that Zeke had made a leap in the dark and split himself in two on the double-bladed axe Uncle Pie had left stuck in the stump that afternoon. Uncle Pie ran back to the cabin with both halves of Zeke and quickly sewed him back together, not even taking time to light the coal oil lantern. Then he put poor Zeke by the fireplace to recuperate. When he lit his lantern, however, Uncle Pie found that he had sewed Zeke's left side on upside-down. Or was it his right side? Anyway, two legs pointed up and two legs pointed down.

Now, you may think that was the end of a great coon dog, but Uncle Pie said when Zeke healed up he was better than ever at running coons because when he got tired of running on two legs, he could just turn a cartwheel and run on the other two for a while.

Another good thing about Zeke was that he never told a lie. The same can't be said for old Uncle Pie.

BACK TROUBLE

(Author's note: I admit that I have shamelessly pilfered the following tale, slightly edited, from a book called *Shoot, Luke, the Air is Full of Pigeons*, by Doc Blakely, my father.)

Way back in the chaparral one night down in the Brush Country, a bunch of hunters were sittin' around the campfire, enjoying a wild game supper of Wolf brand chili, soda crackers, and Colorado kool-aid, when some of the older hunters started giving instructions to the youngsters.

". . . and, son, always look for fresh deer pellets," one old-timer was saying.

"But how can you tell if they're fresh?" a youngster asked.

"It's fresh if it's still rollin' and smokin'."

"Can you tell a new track from an old one?" asked another kid, fascinated by the old codger's knowledge.

"Sure."

"How?"

"Well, sometimes if you look up real fast, you'll see a deer still standin' in 'em."

The youngsters wanted to know more, so the stories really started to fly. One hunter told about his bird dog who was so smart that while he was being paper trained, he learned to read.

The next guy started bragging about his duck-calling skills. Said he made such realistic mating calls that he had to shoot drakes in self-defense.

"Did I tell y'all about that big ol' buck I shot at this morning?" the next fellow asked, throwing a chunk of mesquite on the fire. "He was way off down a sendero, followin' right behind a doe, just as close to her as he could get. I fired once and the doe ran off, but that big ol' buck just stood there. I tried to shoot again, but my rifle jammed, and I started cussin', but to my surprise that big buck still just stood there. Well, I got curious then and walked down the sendero to have a look at him. Found him standin' there with that doe's tail in his mouth. She had been leadin' him around until I shot her tail off. The ol' boy was blind, you see, and didn't know which way to go. I didn't have the heart to kill him."

"That reminds me of a big buck I tracked down one season," said another hunter across the campfire. "I trailed him for weeks and finally discovered that he only came out at night to feed. During the day, he slept in the safest place he could find, in plain sight at a truck stop, stretched across the fender of an abandoned Buick."

About this time, the professional Indian hunting guide hired by the party, Big Bucks Goquickly, stood up to enter the contest. "That's nothing. I was given an old rusty rifle and one bullet when I was about as old as you boys," he said to the youngsters. "My grandfather showed me a set of rabbit tracks and told me I could find supper where they ended.

"The rabbit tried every trick to throw me off his trail, even swimming underwater across a stream. I was following his faint underwater tracks, when in midstream, I saw a flock of geese flying west. I took aim, then saw a flock of ducks flying east. Then I saw a big buck to the north, over to my left. Suddenly another appeared slightly to the right of him.

"I had to make the most of my one shot, so I took careful aim at a rock between the two deer. When I pulled the trigger, the old gun exploded. Half the barrel flew into the geese, killing seven. The other half knocked down eight ducks. The bullet sped true to its mark, splitting in half on the rock, each half dropping a buck deer. The stock flew back, knocking me down in the stream. When I came up, I had a beaver by the tail in each hand, and my pockets were so full of mountain trout that the strain on my pants caused a button to pop off with such force it killed the rabbit."

Now, this blatant absurdity somewhat riled Winston, the best story-teller in camp, so he branched out and told some windy ones about his many hair-raising escapes from dangerous wild animals. One time in Arizona, he had grabbed a ten-foot rattlesnake by the tail and popped its head off. He had killed a polar bear in Alaska armed only with an icicle. Then there was the time in Canada he had single-handedly downed a charging bull moose by hitting him between the eyes with a can of Spam.

After he had put our guide, Big Bucks Goquickly, back in his place, Winston stalked into his Winnebago and went to bed.

Just when the rest of the hunters were ready to turn in, they heard a blood-chilling scream in the night that they all recognized as that of a panther. "Let's get him before he gets away!" one of the boy's shouted, and the race was on, kids and adults running every which way to bag the cat.

"Get up, Winston!" somebody yelled. "There's a panther out here in the dark!"

With guns and flashlights and all the paraphernalia of modern warfare, the hunters charged into the night. An hour later, they returned empty-handed to camp, only to discover that Winston had never left his Winnebago.

"Why didn't you come with us, Winston?" yelled one of the guys through the wall of the camper.

"Back trouble," Winston replied.

"What do you mean, 'back trouble'?"

"This yellow streak down the middle of it is holding me to the mattress!"

TEXAS GHOST TALES

The conversation turned to ghosts.

I was a stranger in Marfa, talking with some of the locals in the lobby of El Paisano Hotel. The old lodge fosters talk of mystery and legend. The stark Spanish architecture, its thick walls, and dark corners seem to lend fitting sanctuary to the wayward residents of limbo.

My companions included the hotel manager, a local entrepreneur, and a couple of itinerant oil field geologists. As night's shadow crept deeper in through the portals of the lobby, mention of the spirit world seemed almost predestined.

"Have you heard about the ghost in this place?" asked one of the straight-faced oilmen. He had sojourned regularly at El Paisano and had firsthand tales to relate. He told how the ghost of the old hotel matron makes her visitations at odd hours of the night, rapping on the doors with her spectral walking stick.

Decades ago, in life, she had been a bitter old woman, perhaps suffering some hidden remorse. She hated to hear joy expressed by a tenant. Laughter ringing from any of the hotel chambers made her charge the scene to silence the uproar by knocking sharply on the door with her cane. After her death, the rappings continued.

The local entrepreneur and the hotel manager concurred with the oilman's story. They had all heard poundings. The second geologist had been near enough to his door one night to open it quickly after the rapping came. He found nothing, though the hall was too long for even a fleet prankster to have escaped unseen.

As I walked down that same corridor to my room, I almost looked forward to hearing the nocturnal reports of the hotel matron's cane.

I don't know at what hour the noises began or how awake they made me. The rapping seemed far away at first. Maybe it was the echo of the lobby conversation in my dreams. But then the din became more deliberate. This was no echo unless it rang from the far walls of oblivion! It sounded like a window shutter flailing in a brief, sudden tempest!

I stayed awake for several minutes, listening. The kitchen was somewhere below me, I reasoned, and the cooks were clamoring, preparing the early breakfasts, perhaps bustling in and out through a kitchen door.

The knocking woke me several more times before dawn, each time sounding farther away. When I rolled out from under the covers, I discovered that the headboard to my bed rattled against the wall when I moved. The sound it made, if amplified by the contrastive stillness of night and reverberated among the images of a rampant imagination, would sound vaguely like an old lady's walking stick banging against a door, I decided.

One of the oilmen asked that morning had I heard the banging? I told him I certainly had. It could have been a loose headboard or a busy kitchen door but, for the benefit of the believers, I attributed the noises to the ghost of the hotel matron.

Thus, the ghost tales of Texas become more vivid with each retelling. Even J. Frank Dobie, master of Texas folklore, once concluded: "If one man does not tell a story—as a story—the way it should be told, the next man is under artistic obligations to improve it."

Here then, for your ghoolish delight, you will find a macabre conclave of Texas ghost stories, many times in the retelling.

House of the Honeymooners

A young bachelor came to Texas in the late 1850s and built a grand plantation house near Brazoria to please his fiancee. In a final architectural flourish, he had his slaves fashion bricks from clay deposits in a nearby creek bed and mortar them into a tall chimney at one end of the house.

The bachelor returned to Tennessee to fetch his bride and bring her to her mansion. Upon arriving, however, he found his betrothed absent from the world, having succumbed to a sudden disease. Shortly, the Civil War began, and the bachelor died in one of its first battles. The mansion near Brazoria would never greet its intended residents—at least not in the flesh.

Other parties tried to occupy the house but found it an unnerving place to live. The doors opened and closed by energies unknown. The front door, especially, remained persistently ajar, as if waiting to receive the rightful owners of the place.

One end of the house collapsed on the last family that tried to make its home there, pinning the husband and wife under debris of the bedroom for several terrifying hours before rescue. Undoubtedly haunted, the house remained vacant thereafter.

Thrill seekers, however, continued to visit the ruins. One of them carved his name on a chimney brick, the soft clay yielding readily to his knife. It became traditional for each brave soul who visited the house to similarly desecrate a brick.

Then the aging chimney began to crumble. The mortar gave way to wind and rain. As each brick returned to dust, so did the person whose name appeared on it. Ghost tempters and brick carvers, of course, ceased to visit and at last the honeymooners had their peace.

The Mountain of Sorrows

A strange light sometimes gleams in the Davis range on a peak called Dolores Mountain. The mountain bears the name of the beautiful, heartbroken village girl whose ghost, they say, now fires the brush on that summit.

In the days when Apaches ruled West Texas, Dolores fell in love with a sheepherder named Jose. Jose was known well for his bravery, for he tended the herds alone for long stretches on the range of the cruel Apache. Dolores feared so for the safety of Jose that she made him agree to a method of communication.

Every evening, she climbed the mountain near her village and lit a fire on its summit. Across the peaks and canyons, wherever his herds might have wandered, Jose stoked a nightly fire in reply to reassure Dolores. For weeks, the firelight flickered every evening across the expanses.

Then one day after dusk Dolores found no blaze to answer hers. She rushed down the mountain to alert her father who rode with other men to find Jose. They found his lifeless body—shot, scalped, and thrown to the bottom of a deep canyon. It was suggested that the sheepherder's fire had brought the Apache down on him.

The light of life in Dolores' eyes died with Jose's last signal fire. Then, to the distress of all who knew her, Dolores resumed her nightly climbs to light the fires. No amount of reason dissuaded her from the ritual. She sat all night, every night, staring across the arid ridges. She died after many thousands of fires had cooled to ash.

The people of the region had grown accustomed to looking for fires on Dolores Mountain—the mountain of sorrows. Even after Dolores died, mysterious fires continued to mark the peak at night. A few climbers who have visited that haunted summit say the dust there, though forever wind-blown, seems strangely discolored by the grey-black cast of ashes.

Four Faces of the Clock

Drive around the courthouse at Gonzales and you will see a clock face on each of four walls high on the brick cupola. Unless the ghost of Albert Howard has loosed his hold on the works of that timepiece, each of its four faces will tell a different minute.

Howard swore his innocence up to the moment of his hanging in 1921. In a courtroom situated below the four faces of the courthouse clock, a jury had found him guilty of rape.

Through the iron-barred window of his prison, Howard could see the north face. A man informed of the date and hour for his own coming demise has little love for the constant passage of time—or any instrument used to measure it. Every circle the hands made drew the noose tighter around Howard's neck until he could no longer bear to regard the clock in silence.

The jailors must have heard Albert Howard curse the timepiece. Soon everyone knew of his vow to visit eternal infirmity upon that instrument after his last fall at the gallows. He swore that no other would ever count the last hours by the sweep of those hands.

The hangman carried out his edict on schedule, and the four faces of the courthouse clock never thereafter agreed. None of them kept time correctly. The interior works were adjusted, then replaced. No amount of tinkering could wrest the gears from the grip of Howard's ghost. And whether by chance or some nameless influence from the afterlife, Gonzales never hanged another soul.

Ghost Dogs of Orozimbo

Not a few Texans wanted Santa Anna executed after his capture at San Jacinto. However, David G. Burnet, the interim president of the Republic, claimed no authority existed for such action. To prevent an assassination, Burnet moved Santa Anna around the settled parts of Texas and kept him chained in leg irons and guarded.

Soon, Santa Anna's chains were heard rattling at the Brazos valley plantation known as Orozimbo, about eleven miles north of present West Columbia. There the prisoner managed to plan an escape with some outside help.

Sometime around Halloween 1836, an enemy of the Republic gave Santa Anna's guards some wine laced with a sleeping potion. When the drug took effect on the Texan guards, Mexican rescuers arrived to free their president. Horses waited in the woods. No mortal hand, it seemed, could prevent the general's escape.

Just as Santa Anna mounted, a trio of hounds arrived. The dogs circled the rescue squad, howling and baying as if under a treed panther. A small detachment of the skeleton Texas army, camping nearby, heard the canine alert and rode to investigate. Santa Anna was soon returned to his chains at Orozimbo.

The patriot dogs, meanwhile, had disappeared. The Texas soldiers searched for them all the next day without luck. They did learn, however, of a former settler near Orozimbo who had owned three good hounds. The owner of the dogs had joined the struggle for Texas Independence and had been executed at the Goliad Massacre by order of Santa Anna. His ghost, it seemed, had followed Santa Anna to Orozimbo to alert the faithful canines.

But the vigilance of the dogs did not end there. Since the night of Santa Anna's thwarted escape, ghost dogs have been glimpsed patrolling the grounds of the old Orozimbo Plantation. Wolf-like, they appear and vanish with greater facility than a deer. They are fated to prowl forever, for their master—after putting them on the trail of Santa Anna—neglected to call them home.

Bailey's Ghost

They say the ghost of Brit Bailey first appeared in 1836, four years after his death. His spectral image floated above his death bed and terrified the new owners of his homestead.

In the 1850s "Bailey's Light" first appeared. It rose from the odd grave under the prairie named for Brit Bailey and hovered among the trees at the prairie's edge. Once, a horseman chased it all night, but couldn't close the distance.

"Old Uncle Bubba," the former slave servant of Brit Bailey, prophesied the ghost-light would appear every seven years. It was reported every seven years up through 1960.

Brit Bailey came to Texas from Kentucky in 1821—two years before Stephen F. Austin's first colonists arrived. Austin didn't recognize Bailey's claim to his homestead along the lower Brazos and gave the land to another settler. Kentucky had convicted Bailey of counterfeiting and Austin wanted him out of the colony. Of course, Brit Bailey refused to go. Austin went to Bailey's Prairie to personally evict the squatter, but backed down to the muzzle of Bailey's rifle.

"Is it not a fact that you once served a term in the Kentucky penitentiary?" the colonizer demanded.

"'Taint that I'm ashamed of," answered Bailey. "It's the term I served on the Kentucky Legislature which sets heavy on my conscience."

Austin never did get along with Bailey, but finally granted him legal claim to his league of land in 1824. Austin also respected Bailey's ability to parley with the local Indians. "Always be friendly, but never back up" was Bailey's credo. He served the colony as an Indian fighter in the 1824

Battle of Jones Creek against the Karankawas, and also fought in the 1832 Battle of Velasco, the first blood-letting between Anglo settlers and Mexican troops.

A few months after that battle, Brit Bailey lay on his deathbed with cholera. In his last days he dictated a will with some strange stipulations. Bailey's coffin went feet-first into an eight-foot shaft, as requested. Instead of "There lies old Bailey," he wanted folks to say, "There stands old Bailey, facing west, rifle and pistols at his side."

Old Uncle Bubba also tried to slip a jug of whiskey into the coffin at his master's secret request. But the widow Bailey found the libation and yanked it from the box. That's why, said Uncle Bubba, old Brit Bailey can't stand easy in his grave. He's still out huntin' that jug of whiskey.

51 14